A SUMMER TO DIE

"Meg's sorrow as well as her joy comes pouring out in this perceptive tale."

—*Booklist*

"Her story [Meg's] captures the mysteries of living and dying without manipulating the reader's emotions, providing understanding and a comforting sense of completion."

—*School Library Journal*

"Appealing . . . brisk, witty, affecting . . . An attractive heroine in an upbeat presentation of a most difficult subject."

—*Kirkus*

A Summer To Die

By Lois Lowry

Illustrated by Jenni Oliver

BANTAM BOOKS
TORONTO · NEW YORK · LONDON

This low-priced Bantam Book
has been completely reset in a type face
designed for easy reading, and was printed
from new plates. It contains the complete
text of the original hard-cover edition.
NOT ONE WORD HAS BEEN OMITTED.

RL 3, IL 4-10

A SUMMER TO DIE

A Bantam Book / published by arrangement with
Houghton Mifflin Company

PRINTING HISTORY

Houghton Mifflin edition published April 1977
2nd printing .... October 1977   3rd printing .... July 1978
Bantam edition / January 1979

ISBN 0-553-11951-6

Published simultaneously in the United States and Canada

Bantam Books are published by Bantam Books, Inc. Its trademark, consisting of the words "Bantam Books" and the por-
trayal of a bantam, is Registered in U.S. Patent and Trademark
Office and in other countries. Marca Registrada. Bantam
Books, Inc., 666 Fifth Avenue, New York, New York 10019.

PRINTED IN THE UNITED STATES OF AMERICA

A Summer
To Die

1

It was Molly who drew the line.

She did it with chalk—a fat piece of white chalk left over from when we lived in town, had sidewalks, and used to play hopscotch, back when we both were younger. That piece of chalk had been around for a long time. She fished it out of a little clay dish that I had made in last year's pottery class, where it was lying with a piece of string and a few paper clips and a battery that we weren't quite sure was dead.

She took the chalk and drew a line right on the rug. Good thing it wasn't a fuzzy rug or it never would have worked; but it was an old, worn, leftover rug from the dining room of our other house: very flat, and the chalk made a perfect white line across the blue—and then, while I watched in amazement (because it was unlike

Molly, to be so angry), she kept right on drawing the line up the wall, across the wallpaper with its blue flowers. She stood on her desk and drew the line up to the ceiling, and then she went back to the other side of the room and stood on her bed and drew the line right up to the ceiling on that wall, too. Very neatly. Good thing it was Molly who drew it; if I had tried, it would have been a mess, a wavy line and off center. But Molly is very neat.

Then she put the chalk back in the dish, sat down on her bed, and picked up her book. But before she started to read again, she looked over at me (I was still standing there amazed, not believing that she had drawn the line at all) and said, "There. Now be as much of a slob as you want, only keep your mess on your side. *This* side is *mine*."

When we lived in town we had our own rooms, Molly and I. It didn't really make us better friends, but it gave us a chance to ignore each other more.

Funny thing about sisters. Well, about us, anyway; Dad says it's unacademic to generalize. Molly is prettier than I am, but I'm smarter than Molly. I want with my whole being to *be* something someday; I like to think that someday, when I'm grown up, people everywhere will know who I am, because I will have accomplished something important—I don't even know for sure yet what I want it to be, just that it will be something that makes people say my name, Meg Chalmers, with respect. When I told Molly that once, she said that what *she* wants is to have a different name when she grows up, to be Molly Something Else, to be Mrs. Somebody, and to have her children, lots of them, call her

2

"Mother," with respect, and that's all she cares about. She's content, waiting for that; I'm restless, and so impatient. She's sure, absolutely sure, that what she's waiting for will happen, just the way she wants it to; and I'm so uncertain, so fearful my dreams will end up forgotten somewhere, someday, like a piece of string and a paper clip lying in a dish.

Being both determined and unsure at the same time is what makes me the way I am, I think: hasty, impetuous, sometimes angry over nothing, often miserable about everything. Being so well sorted out in her own goals, and so assured of everything happening the way she wants and expects it to, is what makes Molly the way she is: calm, easygoing, self-confident, downright smug.

Sometimes it seems as if, when our parents created us, it took them two tries, two daughters, to get all the qualities of one whole, well-put-together person. More often, though, when I think about it, I feel as if they got those qualities on their first try, and I represent the leftovers. That's not a good way to feel about yourself, especially when you know, down in the part of you where the ambition is, where the dreams are, where the logic lies, that it's not true.

The hardest part about living in the same room with someone is that it's hard to keep anything hidden. I don't mean the unmatched, dirty socks or the fourteen crumpled papers with tries at an unsuccessful poem on them, although those are the things that upset Molly, that made her draw the line. I mean the parts of yourself that are private: the tears you want to shed sometimes for no reason, the thoughts you want to think in a solitary place, the words you want to say aloud to hear how they sound, but only to yourself. It's important to have a place to close a door on those things, the way I did in town.

The house in town is still there, and it's still our house, but there are other people living in it now, which does something terrible to my stomach when I think about it too much. My room had red-and-white-checked wallpaper; there is a place in one corner, by a window, where I played three games of tick-tack-toe on the wallpaper with a Magic Marker. Cats' games, all of them. I played against myself, so it didn't matter much, but it's funny, how you want to win anyway.

The university clock in its high brick tower was just across the street from the house; at night, when I was supposed to be sleeping I could hear it strike each hour, the chimes coming clear and well defined as silhouettes from the ivied circle of the numbered face in the dark. That's one of the things I miss most, living out here in the country, out here in the middle of nowhere. I like quiet. And it sure is quiet here. But there are times when I lie awake at night and all I can hear is Molly breathing in the bed next to mine; cars seldom go past on this road, and no clocks strike, nothing measures the moments. There is just this quiet, and it seems lonely.

The quiet is why we came. The university has given my dad just this year to finish his book. He worked on it for a while in the old house, shut in his study; but even though he was officially on leave from teaching, the students kept stopping by. "I just thought I'd drop in for a minute to see Dr. Chalmers," they'd say, standing on the porch, looking embarrassed. My

4

mother would say, "Dr. Chalmers can't be disturbed," and then my father's voice would call from upstairs, "Let them in, Lydia, I want to stop for coffee anyway."

So my mother would bring them in, and they would stay for hours, having coffee, talking to Dad, and then he would invite them for dinner, and Mother would add some noodles to the casserole, wash another head of lettuce for the salad, or quickly peel a few more carrots for the stew. We would take hours eating, because everyone talked so much, and my father would open a bottle of wine. Sometimes it would be late at night before they left. I would be in bed by then, listening to the clock chime across the street as they said good-bye on the porch, lingering to ask questions, to exhaust an argument, to laugh at another of my father's anecdotes. Then I would hear my parents come upstairs to bed, and I would hear my father say, "Lydia, I am *never* going to finish this book."

The title of the book is *The Dialectic Synthesis of Irony*. When Dad announced that, very proud of it, at dinner one night, Mom asked, "Can you say that three times fast?" Molly and I tried, and couldn't, and it broke us up. Dad looked very stern, and said, "It is going to be a very important book"; Molly said, "What is?" and he tried to say the title again, couldn't, and it broke him up, too.

He tried to explain to me once what the title means, but he gave up. Molly said *she* understood it very well. But Molly is full of bull sometimes.

It was at breakfast the Saturday morning before Thanksgiving that Mom and Dad told us we were leaving the house in town. I had figured that something was going on, because my moth-

5

er had been on the phone all week, and my mother is not the type of woman who talks on the phone very much.

"We've found a house," Mom said, pouring more coffee for herself and Dad, "out in the country so that your father can have some peace and quiet. It's a lovely house, girls, built in 1840, with a big fireplace in the kitchen. It's on a dirt road, and surrounded by one hundred sixty acres of woods and fields. When summer comes we'll be able to put in a vegetable garden—"

Summer. I guess Molly and I had been thinking the same thing, that she was talking about a month or so, maybe till after Christmas vacation. But *summer.* It was only November. We sat there like idiots, with our mouths open. I had been *born* while we lived in the house in town, thirteen years before, and now they were talking about leaving it behind. I couldn't think of anything to say, which is not unusual for me. But Molly always thinks of things to say.

"What about school?" she asked.

"You'll go by bus, to the Macwahoc Valley Consolidated School. It's a good school, and it's only about a twenty-minute bus ride."

"Can you say that three times fast?" asked Dad, grinning. "Macwahoc Valley Consolidated School?" We didn't even try.

Consolidated school. I didn't even know what that meant. To be honest, it sounded to me as if the school needed a laxative. Anyway, school wasn't my main concern. I was thinking about my Thursday afternoon art class, which was just about to get into oils after umpteen weeks on watercolors, and my Saturday morning photography class, where my photograph of the clock tower at sunset had just been selected Best

6

of the Week, beating out the eight others in the class, which were all taken by boys.

But I didn't even ask about my classes, about what would happen to them when we moved to the country. Because I knew.

"Dad," groaned Molly. "I've just made *cheerleader*."

Boy, was that the wrong thing to say to my father. He's proud of Molly, because she's pretty and all that, even though he always seems somewhat surprised by her, that all of a sudden since she turned fifteen, she has boyfriends and stuff. Every now and then he looks at her and shakes his head in a kind of astonishment, and pride. But he has this thing about priorities, and when Molly said that, he set down his coffee cup very hard and looked at her with a frown.

"Cheerleading," he said, "does not have top priority."

And that was that. It was all decided, and there wasn't anything to argue or fuss about. It was too busy a time, anyway. We almost skipped Thanksgiving, except that there were students who couldn't go home for the vacation, and so five of them spent that Thursday with us, and Mom cooked a turkey. But most of the day we packed. The students helped to put books into boxes, and some of them helped Mom, packing dishes and kitchen things. I did all my packing alone that week. I cried when I fitted my new, unused box of oil paints—a gift for my thirteenth birthday the month before—into a box, and I cried again when I packed my camera. But at least those things, the things I cared about most, were going with me. Molly had to give her blue and white cheerleading outfit to one of the substitute cheerleaders, a girl named Lisa

7

Halstead, who pretended to be sad and sympathetic, but you could tell it was phony; she couldn't wait to get home and try on that pleated skirt.

And all of that was only last month. It seems like a hundred years ago.

Strange, how the age of a house makes a difference. That shouldn't surprise me, because certainly the age of a person makes a big difference, like with Molly and me. Molly is fifteen, which means that she puts on eyeshadow when Mom doesn't catch her at it, and she spends hours in front of the mirror arranging her hair different ways; she stands sideways there, too, to see what her figure looks like, and she talks on the phone every evening to friends, mostly about boys. It took her about two days to make friends in the new school, two days after that to have boyfriends, and the next week she was chosen as a substitute cheerleader.

Me, I'm only two years younger, and that seems to make such a difference, though I haven't figured out why. It's not only physical, although that's part of it. If I stand sideways in front of a mirror—which I don't bother doing—I might as well be standing backwards, for all the difference it makes. And I couldn't begin to put on eyeshadow even if I wanted to, because I can't see without my glasses. Those are the physical things; the real difference seems to be that I don't care about those things. Will I, two years from now? Or do I care now, and pretend I don't, even to myself? I can't figure it out.

As for friends? Well, the first day at the consolidated school, when the first teacher said, "Margaret Chalmers" and I told him, "Would you call me Meg, please," a boy on the side of

8

the classroom called out, "Nutmeg!" Now, three weeks later, there are 323 people in the Macwahoc Valley Consolidated School who call me Nutmeg Chalmers. You know the old saying about with friends like that, who needs enemies?

But I was talking about the age of houses. As my mother had said, this house was built in 1840. That makes it almost one hundred and forty years old. Our house in town was fifty years old. The difference is that the house in town was big, with a million closets and stairways and windows and an attic, all sorts of places for privacy and escape: places where you could curl up with a book and no one would know you were there for hours. Places that were just mine, like the little alcove at the top of the attic stairs, where I tacked my photographs and watercolors on the wall to make my own private gallery, and no one bugged me about the thumbtack holes in the wall.

It's important, I think, to have places like that in your life, secrets that you share only by choice. I said that to Molly once, and she didn't understand; she said she would like to share everything. It's why she likes cheerleading, she said: because she can throw out her arms and a whole crowd of people responds to her.

Here, in the country, the house is very small. Dad explained that it was built this way because it was so hard to keep it warm way back then. The ceilings are low; the windows are small; the staircase is like a tiny tunnel. Nothing seems to fit right. The floors slant, and there are wide spaces between the pine boards. If you close a door, it falls open again all on its own, when you're not looking. It doesn't matter much, the doors not closing, because there's no

place for privacy anyway. Why bother to close
the door to your room when it's not even your
own room?

When we got here, I ran inside the empty
house while the others were all still standing in
the yard, trying to help the moving van get
turned around in the snowy driveway. I went up
the little flight of stairs, looked around, and saw
the three bedrooms: two big ones, and the tiny
one in the middle, just off the narrow hall. In
that room the ceiling was slanted almost down to
the floor, and there was one window that looked
out over the woods behind the house, and the
wallpaper was yellow, very faded and old but
still yellow, with a tiny green leaf here and there
in the pattern. There was just room for my
bed and my desk and my bookcase and the few
other things that would make it really mine. I
stood for a long time by that one window, looking out at the woods. Across a field to the left
of the house, I could see another house far away;
it was empty, the outside unpainted, and the
windows, some of them broken, black like dark
eyes. The rectangle of the window in the little
room was like the frame of a painting, and I
stood there thinking how I would wake up
each morning there, looking out, and each day it
would change to a new kind of picture. The snow
would get deeper; the wind would blow those
last few leaves from the trees; there would be
icicles hanging from the edge of the roof; and
then, in spring, things would melt, and change,
and turn green. There would be rabbits in the
field in the early morning. Wild flowers. Maybe
someone would come to live in that abandoned
house, and light would come from those dark
windows at night, across the meadow.

Finally I went downstairs. My mother was in

the empty living room, figuring out how to fit in the big couch from the other house. Dad and Molly were still outside, sprinkling salt on the driveway so that the moving men wouldn't slip on the snow.

"Mom," I said, "the little room is mine, isn't it?"

She stopped to think for a minute, remembering the upstairs of the new house. Then she put her arm around me and said, "Meg, the little room is for Dad's study. That's where he'll finish the book. You and Molly will share the big bedroom at the end of the hall, the one with the pretty blue-flowered wallpaper."

Mom always tried to make things right with gestures: hugs, quick kisses blown across a room, waves, winks, smiles. Sometimes it helps.

I went back upstairs, to the big room that wasn't going to be all mine. From the windows I could still see the woods, and part of the empty house across the field, but the view was partly blocked by the big gray falling-down barn that was attached to our house on the side. It wasn't the same. I'm pretty good at making the best of things, but it wasn't the same.

Now, just a month later, just two days before Christmas, the house looks lived in. It's warm, and full of the sound of fires in the fireplaces, the sound of Dad's typewriter upstairs, and full of winter smells like wet boots drying, and cinnamon, because my mother is making pumpkin pies and gingerbread. But now Molly, who wants more than anything to throw out her arms and share, has drawn that line, because I can't be like those crowds who smile at her, and share back.

2

Good things are happening here. That surprises me a little. When we came, I thought it would be a place where I would just have to stick it out, where I would be lonely for a year. Where nothing would ever happen at all.

Now good things are happening to all of us. Well, it's hard to tell with my mother; she's the kind of person who always enjoys everything anyway. Molly and Mom are a lot alike. They get so enthusiastic and excited that you think something wonderful has happened; then, when you stop to think about it, nothing has really happened at all. Every morning, for example, Mom puts fresh birdseed in the bird feeder outside the kitchen window. Two minutes later the first bird stops by for breakfast, and Mom jumps up, says "Shhh" and goes to look, and you forget that

400 birds were there the day before. Or a plant in the kitchen gets a new leaf and she almost sends out birth announcements. So it always seems as if good things are happening to Mom.

Dad is more like me; he waits for the truly good things, as if getting excited about the little ones might keep the big ones from coming. But the book is going well for Dad, and he says it was coming here that did it.

He goes into the little room each morning, closes the door, and sets a brick against it so that it won't fall open while he's working. He's still there when Molly and I get home from school at four, and Mom says he doesn't come out all day, except every now and then when he appears in the kitchen and pours himself a cup of coffee without saying a word, and goes back upstairs. Like a sleepwalker, Mom says. We can hear the typewriter going full speed; every now and then we hear him rip up or crumple a piece of paper, and then roll a fresh one into the typewriter and start clattering away again. He talks to himself, too—we can hear him muttering behind the door—but talking to himself is a good sign. When he's silent, it means things aren't going well, but he's been talking to himself behind the door to the little room ever since we came here.

Last night he came to dinner looking very preoccupied, but smiling to himself now and then. Molly and I were talking about school, and Mom was telling us how she had decided to make a patchwork quilt while we're living in the country, using scraps of material from all the clothes Molly and I wore when we were little. We started remembering our old dresses—we don't even *wear* dresses anymore; I don't think I've worn anything but jeans for two years.

Molly said, "Remember that yucky dress I used to have that had butterflies on it? The one I wore at my sixth birthday party?" I didn't remember it, but Mom did; she laughed, and said, "Molly, that was a *beautiful* dress. Those butterflies were hand-embroidered! It's going into a special place on the quilt!"

Dad hadn't heard a word, but he'd been sitting there with a half-smile on his face. All of a sudden he said, "Lydia, I really have a grip on Coleridge!" and he jumped up from his chair, leaving half a piece of apple pie, and went back to the study, taking the stairs two at a time. We could hear the typewriter start up again.

Mom looked after him with that special fond look she gives to things that are slightly foolish and very lovable. She smiles, and her eyes look as if they can see back into her memory, into all the things that have gone into making a person what they are. With Dad, I think she looks back to when she knew him as a student, when he must have been serious and forgetful and very kind, the way he still is, but young, which he isn't anymore. With me, I know her memories go back to all sorts of frustrations and confusions, because I was never an "easy" child; I remember that I questioned and argued and raged. But her look, for me, is still that same caring look that goes beyond all that. As for Molly? I've seen her look at Molly that way, too, and it's a more complicated thing; I think when Mom looks at Molly, her memories go back farther, to her own self as a girl, because they are so alike, and it must be a puzzling thing to see yourself growing up again. It must be like looking through the wrong end of a telescope—seeing yourself young, far away, on your own; the distance is too great for the watcher, really, to do anything more than watch, and remember, and smile.

Molly has a boyfriend. Boys have *always* liked Molly. When she was little, boys in the neighborhood used to come to repair her bike; they loaned her their skate keys, brought her home when she skinned her knees and waited, anxious, while she got a Band-Aid; they shared their trick-or-treat candy with Molly at Halloween. When I was down to the dregs in my paper bag, two weeks later, down to eating the wrinkled apples in the bottom, Molly always had Mounds bars left, gifts from the boys on the block.

How could boys *not* like a girl who looks the way she does? I've gotten used to Molly's looks because I've lived with her for thirteen years. But every now and then I glance at her and see her as if she were a stranger. One night recently she was sitting in front of the fire doing her homework, and I looked over because I wanted to ask her a question about negative numbers. The light from the fire was on her face, all gold, and her blond hair was falling down across her forehead and in waves around her cheeks and onto her shoulders. For a second she looked just like a picture on a Christmas card we had gotten from friends in Boston; it was almost eerie. I held my breath when I looked at her for that moment, because she looked so beautiful. Then she saw me watching her, and stuck her tongue out, so that she was just Molly again, and familiar.

Boys, I think, probably see that part of her all the time, the beautiful part. And now suddenly this one boy, Tierney McGoldrick, who plays on the basketball team and is also president of the junior class, is hanging around her every minute in school. They're always together, and he lets her wear his school jacket with a big MV for Macwahoc Valley on the back. Of course, because we live out here in the middle of the woods, so far from everything, they can't actually date. Tierney's not old enough to drive, even if he wanted to drive all the way from where he lives; half the distance is a dirt road that's usually covered with snow. But he calls her up every single night. Molly takes the phone into the pantry, so that the long cord is stretched all across the kitchen, and my mother and I have to step over it while we're putting the dinner dishes away. Mom thinks it's quite funny. But then Mom has curly hair too, and was probably just as beautiful as Molly once. Maybe it's because I have straight stringy hair and glasses that the whole thing makes me feel a little sad.

So Dad has a grip on Coleridge, whatever that means, and Molly has a grip on Tierney McGoldrick. Me, I can't actually say I have a grip on anything, but good things have been happening to me here, too.

I have a new friend.

Just after New Year's, before school vacation ended, I went out for a walk. It was a walk I'd been meaning to take ever since we moved to the house, but things had been so busy, first with school and fixing up the house, then Christmas, then settling down after Christmas—I don't know, the time just never seemed right for it. I guess I like to think that it was fate that sent me out for this particular walk on this particular day. Fate, and the fact that the sun finally came out after weeks of grayness and snow.

I took my camera—the first time I'd taken my camera out since we came to the country—and went, all bundled up in my down jacket and wearing heavy boots, down the dirt road beyond our house. I walked toward the abandoned house that I could see across the fields from the upstairs window.

The snow kept me from getting close to it. The house is a long distance back from the road and of course the driveway, really a narrow road in its own right, hadn't been plowed. But I stood, stamping my feet to keep warm, and looked at it for a long time. It reminds me of a very honest and kind blind man. That sounds silly. But it looks honest to me because it's so square and straight. It's a very old house—I know that because of the way it's built, with a center chimney and all the other things I've learned about from living in *our* old house—but its corners are all square like a man holding his shoulders straight. Nothing sags on it at all. It's a shabby house, though, with no paint, so that the old boards are all weathered to gray. I guess that's why it seems kind, because it doesn't mind being poor and paintless; it even seems to be proud of it. Blind because it doesn't look back at me. The windows are empty and dark. Not scary. Just waiting, and thinking about something.

I took a couple of photographs of the house from the road and walked on. I know the dirt road ends a mile beyond our house, but I had never gone to the end. The school bus turns around in our driveway, and no other cars ever come down this road except for one beat-up truck now and then.

That same truck was parked at the end of the road, beside a tiny, weatherbeaten house that looked like a distant, poorer cousin of the one I'd passed. An elderly cousin, frail but very proud. There was smoke coming out of the chimney, and curtains in the two little windows on either side of the door. A dog in the yard, who thumped his tail against a snowbank when he saw me coming. And beside the truck—no, actually in the truck, or at least with his head inside it, under the hood, was a man.

"Hi," I called. It would have been silly to turn around and start walking home without saying anything, even though I've promised my parents all my life that I would never talk to strange men.

He lifted out his head, a gray head, with a bright red woolen cap on it, smiled—a nice smile—and said, "Miss Chalmers. I'm glad you've come to visit."

"Meg," I said automatically. I was puzzled. How did he know who I was? Our name isn't even on the mailbox.

"For Margaret?" he asked, coming over and shaking my hand, or at least my mitten, leaving a smear of grease on it. "Forgive me. My hands are very dirty. My battery dies in this cold weather."

"How did you know?"

"How did I know Meg for Margaret? Because Margaret was my wife's name; therefore, one of my favorite names, of course. And I called her Meg at times, though no one else did."

"They call me Nutmeg at school. I bet no one ever called your wife Nutmeg."

He laughed. He had beautiful blue eyes, and his face moved into a new pattern of wrinkles when he laughed. "No," he admitted, "they didn't. But she wouldn't have minded. Nutmeg was one of her favorite spices. She wouldn't have made an apple pie without it."

"What I meant, though, when I said, 'How

18

did you know?' was how did you know my name was Chalmers?"

He wiped his hands on a greasy rag that was hanging from the door handle of the truck. "My dear, I apologize. I have not even introduced myself. My name is Will Banks. And it's much too cold to stand out here. Your toes must be numb, even in those boots. Come inside, and I'll make us each a cup of tea. And I'll tell you how I know your name."

I briefly envisioned myself telling my mother, "So then I went in his house," and I briefly envisioned my mother saying, "You went in his *house?*"

He saw me hesitate, and smiled. "Meg," he said, "I'm seventy years old. Thoroughly harmless, even to a beautiful young girl like you. Come on in and keep me company for a bit, and get warm."

I laughed, because he knew what I was thinking, and very few people ever know what I'm thinking. Then I went in his house.

What a surprise. It was a tiny house, and very old, and looked on the outside as if it might fall down any minute. For that matter, his truck was also very old, and looked as if *it* might fall down any minute. And Mr. Banks himself was old, although he didn't appear to be falling apart.

But inside, the house was beautiful. Everything was perfect, as if it were a house I'd imagined, or dreamed up with a set of paints. There were only two rooms on the first floor. On one side of the little front hall was the living room: the walls were painted white, and there was an oriental rug on the floor, all shades of blues and reds. A big fireplace, with a painting

19

that was a real painting, not a print, hanging over the mantel. A pewter pitcher standing on a polished table. A large chest of drawers with bright brass handles. A wing chair that was all done in needlepoint—all done by hand, I could tell, because my mother does needlepoint sometimes. Sunlight was pouring in the little windows, through the white curtains, making patterns on the rug and chairs.

On the other side of the hall was the kitchen. That's where Mr. Banks and I went, after he had shown me the living room. A wood stove was burning in the kitchen, and a copper kettle sat on top of it, steaming. A round pine table was laid with woven blue mats, and in the center of it a blue and white bowl held three apples like a still life. Everything was scrubbed and shiny and in the right place.

It made me think of a song that we sang in kindergarten, when we sat at our desks and folded our hands. "We're all in our places with bright shiny faces," we used to sing. I could hear the words in my mind, the little voices of all those five-year-olds, and it was a good memory; Mr. Banks' house was like that, a house warm with memories, of things in their places, and smiling.

He took my jacket and hung it up with his, and poured tea into two thick pottery mugs. We sat at the table, in pine chairs that gleamed almost yellow from a combination of old wood, polish, and sunlight.

"Is yours the little room at the top of the stairs?" he asked me.

How did he know about the little room? "No," I explained. "I wanted it to be. It's so perfect. You can see the other house across the field, you know"—he nodded; he knew "—but my father needed that room. He's writing a book. So my sister and I have the big room together."

"The little room was mine," he said, "when I was a small boy. Sometime when your father isn't working there, go in and look in the closet. On the closet floor you'll find my name carved, if no one's refinished the floor. My mother spanked me for doing it. I was eight years old at the time, and I'd been shut in my room for being rude to my older sister."

"You lived in my house?" I asked in surprise.

He laughed again. "My dear Meg," he said, "*you* live in *my* house.

"My grandfather built that house. Actually, he built the one across the field, first. Then he built the other one, where you live. In those days families stuck together, of course, and he built the second house for his sister, who never married. Later he gave it to his oldest son—my father—and my sister and I were both born there.

"It became my house when I married Margaret. I took her there to live when she was a bride, eighteen years old. My sister had married and moved to Boston. She's dead now. My parents, of course, are gone. And Margaret and I never had children. So there's no one left but me. Well, that's not entirely true—there's my sister's son, but that's another story.

"Anyway, there's no one left here on the land but me. There were times, when I was young, when Margaret was with me, when I was tempted to leave, to take a job in a city, to make a lot of money, but—" He lit his pipe, was quiet for a minute, looking into the past.

"Well, it was my grandfather's land, and my father's, before it was mine. Not many people understand that today, what that means. But I *know* this land. I know every rock, every tree. I couldn't leave them behind.

"This house used to be the hired man's cottage. I've fixed it up some, and it's a good little house. But the other two houses are still mine. When the taxes went up, I just couldn't afford to keep them going. I moved here after Margaret died, and I've rented the family houses whenever I come across someone who has reason to want to live in this wilderness.

"When I heard your parents were looking for a place, I offered the little house to them. It's a perfect place for a writer—the solitude stimulates imagination, I think.

"Other people come now and then, thinking it might be a cheap place to live, but I won't rent to just anyone. That's why the big house is empty now—the right family hasn't come along."

"Do you get lonely here?"

He finished his tea and set the cup down on the table. "No. I've been here all my life. I miss my Margaret, of course. But I have Tip"—the dog looked up at his name, and thumped his tail against the floor—"and I do some carpentry in the village now and then, when people need me. I have books. That's all I need, really.

"Of course," he smiled, "it's nice to have a new friend, like you."

"Mr. Banks?"

"Oh please, please. Call me Will, the way all my friends do."

"Will, then. Would you mind if I took your picture?"

"My dear," he said, straightening his shoulders and buttoning the top button of his plaid shirt. "I would be honored."

The light was coming in through the kitchen

22

window onto his face: soft light now; it had become late afternoon, when all the harsh shadows are gone. He sat right there, smoked his pipe, and talked, and I finished the whole roll of film, just shooting quickly as he gestured and smiled. All those times when I feel awkward and inept—all those times are made up for when I have my camera, when I can look through the viewfinder and feel that I can control the focus and the light and the composition, when I can capture what I see, in a way that no one else is seeing it. I felt that way while I was taking Will's picture.

I unloaded the exposed film and carried it home in my pocket like a secret. When I looked back from the road, Will was by his truck again, waving to me; Tip was back by his snowbank, thumping his tail.

And deep, way deep inside me somewhere was something else that kept me warm on the walk home, even though the sun was going down and the wind was coming over the piles of snow on either side of the road, blowing stinging powder into my eyes. It was the fact that Will Banks had called me beautiful.

3

February is the worst month, in New England. I think so, anyway. My mother doesn't agree with me. Mom says April is, because everything turns to mud in April; the snow melts, and things that were buried all winter—dog messes, lost mittens, beer bottles tossed from cars—all reappear, still partly frozen into icy mixtures that are half the gray remains of old snow and half the brown beginnings of mud. Lots of the mud, of course, ends up on the kitchen floor, which is why my mother hates April.

My father, even though he always recites a poem that begins "April is the cruelest month" to my mother when she's scrubbing the kitchen floor in the spring, agrees with me that it's February that's worst. Snow, which was fun in December, is just boring, dirty, and downright cold in February. And the same sky that was blue in January is just nothing but white a month later—so white that sometimes you can't tell where the sky ends and the land begins. And it's cold, bitter cold, the kind of cold where you just can't go outside. I haven't been to see Will, because it's too cold to walk a mile up the road. I haven't taken any pictures, because it's too cold to take off my mittens and operate the camera.

And Dad can't write. He goes in the little room and sits, every day, but the typewriter is quiet. It's almost noisy, the quietness, we are all so aware of it. He told me that he sits and looks out the window at all the whiteness and I can't get a grip on anything. I understand that; if I were able to go out with my camera in the cold, the film wouldn't be able to grip the edges and corners of things because everything has blended so into the colorless, stark mass of February. For Dad, everything has blended into a mass without any edges in his mind, and he can't write.

I showed him the closet floor, where *William* is carved into the pine.

"Will Banks is a fascinating man," Dad said, leaning back in his scruffy leather chair in front of the typewriter. He was having a cup of coffee, and I had tea. It was the first time I had visited him in the little room, and he seemed glad to have company. "You know, he's well educated, and he's a master cabinetmaker. He could have earned a fortune in Boston, or New York, but he wouldn't leave this land. People around here think he's a little crazy. But I don't know, I don't know."

"He's not crazy, Dad. He's nice. But it's too bad he has to live in that teeny house, when he owns both these bigger ones that were his family's."

"Well, he's happy there, Meg, and you can't argue with happiness. Problem is, there's a nephew in Boston who's going to make trouble for Will, I'm afraid."

"What do you mean? How can anyone make trouble for an old man who isn't bothering anybody?"

"I'm not sure. I wish I knew more about law. Seems the nephew is the only relative he has. Will owns all this land, and the houses—they were left to him—but when he dies, they'll go to this nephew, his sister's son. It's valuable property. They may not look like much to you, Meg, but these houses are real antiques, the kind of things that a lot of people from big cities would like to buy. The nephew, apparently, would like to have Will declared what the law calls 'incompetent'—which just means crazy. If he could do that, he'd have control over the property. He'd like to sell it to some people who want to build cottages for tourists, and to turn the big house into an inn."

I stood up and looked out the window, across the field, to where the empty house was standing gray against the whiteness, with its brick chimney tall and straight against the sharp line of the roof. I imagined cute little blue shutters on the windows, and a sign over the door that said "All Major Credit Cards Accepted." I envisioned a parking lot, filled with cars and campers from different states.

"They can't do that, Dad," I said. Then it turned into a question. "Can they?"

My father shrugged. "I didn't think so. But last week the nephew called me, and asked if it were true, what he had heard, that the people in the village call Will 'Loony Willie.' "

" '*Loony Willie*'? What did you say to him?"

"I told him I'd never heard anything so ridiculous in my life, and to stop bothering me, because I was busy writing a book that was going to change the whole history of literature."

That broke us both up. The book that was going to change the whole history of literature was lying in stacks all over my father's desk, on the floor, in at least a hundred crumpled sheets of typing paper in the big wastebasket, and in two pages that he had made into paper airplanes and sailed across the room. We laughed and laughed.

When I was able to stop laughing, I remembered something that I had wanted to tell my father. "You know, last month, when I visited Will, I took his picture."

"Mmmmm?"

"He was sitting in his kitchen, smoking his pipe and looking out the window, and talking. I shot a whole roll. And you know, Dad, his eyes are so bright, and his face is so alive, so full of memories and thoughts. He's interested in everything. I thought of that when you said Loony Willie."

"Could I see the pictures?"

I felt a little silly. "Well, I haven't been able to develop them yet, Dad. I can't use the darkroom at school because I have to catch the early bus to get home. It's just that I *remember* his face looking like that when I photographed him."

My father sat up straight in his chair very suddenly. "Meg," he said, "I have a *great* idea!" He sounded like a little boy. Once Mom told Molly and me that she didn't mind not having sons, because often Dad is like a little boy, and now I could see exactly what she meant. He looked as if he were ten years old, on a Saturday morning, with an exciting and probably impossible project in mind.

"Let's build a darkroom!" he said.

I could hardly believe it. *"Here?"* I asked.

"Why not? Now look, I don't know anything about photography. You'll be the expert consultant. But I *do* know how to build. And I need a little vacation from writing. Could I do it in a week?"

"Sure, I think so."

"What would you need?"

"A space, first of all."

"How about that little storeroom in the passageway between the house and the barn? That's big enough, isn't it?"

"Sure. But it's too cold, Dad."

"Aha. You're not thinking, Consultant. We need a heater." He turned to his desk, found a fresh sheet of paper, and wrote, "1. Heater." My father loves to make lists. "What next?"

"Let's see. There are already shelves in there. But I'd need a counter top of some sort." He wrote that down.

"And special lights. They're called safelights. You know, so you won't expose the photographic paper accidentally."

"No problem. There's electricity out there. What else? You'll need lots of equipment, won't you? If you're going to have a darkroom, it might as well be the best darkroom around."

I sighed. I could already tell what the problem was going to be. But, as I said, my father loves making lists. What the heck. I started telling him everything a darkroom would need: an enlarger, a

28

timer, trays, chemicals, paper, developing tanks, special thermometers, filters, a focuser. The list grew very long and he started on a second sheet of paper. It was kind of fun, listing it, even though I knew it was just a dream. It was a dream I'd had for a long time, one that I'd never told anyone.

"Where can you get this kind of stuff?" he asked.

I went to my room, picked out one of my photography magazines, and brought it back. We looked through the ads in the back pages: New York. California. Boston.

"Boston," he said triumphantly. "Terrific. I have to go down there to see my publisher anyway; might as well do it this week." He wrote down the name and address of the company. "Now, How much is all of this going to cost?"

I started to laugh, even though I didn't really feel like laughing. It was so typical of my father, that he didn't think of the obvious problem till last. We looked through the Boston company's price list, wrote the prices on my father's paper, and finally added them up. His face fell. Good thing I'd realized all along it was a dream; that made it less disappointing. Poor Dad; he'd thought it was real, and it took him by surprise that it wasn't.

We both kept smiling very hard, because neither of us wanted the other to be sad.

"Listen, Meg," he said slowly, folding the list up and putting it on a corner of his desk. "Sometimes when I'm sitting here working on the book, I come to a problem that seems insurmountable. When that happens, I just let it go for a while. I keep it in the back of my mind, but I don't *agonize* over it. Do you know what I mean?"

I nodded. I'm pretty good at not agonizing.

"So far," he explained, "all of those problems have resolved themselves. Out of nowhere, all of a

29

sudden, the solutions appear. Now here's what I want you to do." He tapped the folded darkroom list with his finger. "I want you to put this out of your mind for a while, but keep it somewhere in the back where your subconscious will be working on it."

"Okay," I agreed.

"And before long, the solution will come. I'm absolutely sure of it. Probably soon, too, because *both* of our subconsciouses will be working."

I laughed. He was so sure, and I didn't believe it for a minute. "All right," I promised.

"Or would that be 'subconsciese'? The plural, I mean?"

"Dad," I said, picking up our empty cups to take them to the kitchen, *"you're* the English professor."

Mom was in the kitchen, sitting by the fireplace stitching on her quilt. She was so excited about that quilt, and it *was* pretty, what she had done so far. But Molly and I cringed when we looked at it too closely, I suppose because it was full of memories; let's face it, some memories are better off forgotten, especially when you haven't lived far enough beyond them yet. There was the dress with the butterflies, which Molly always hated, right near the center. Near it was a blue-and-white-striped piece that I didn't want to be reminded of. It was the dress that I wore to my fifth birthday party, the day when I threw up all over the table, just after the cake was served. There was the pink with little white flowers, that I wore to Sunday School on Easter when I was supposed to say a poem to a roomful of people, forgot every word of it, and cried instead, when I was maybe six. There was the blue plaid that Molly wore her first day in junior high, when she didn't realize that every other girl would be wearing

30

jeans. And there was a piece of my old Brownie uniform; I hated Brownies, always spent my dues on candy before I got there, and was scolded every week.

"What's that white piece with the embroidery?" I asked Mom. She really liked it when Molly and I took an interest in the quilt.

She turned the quilt around and held it toward the window so that she could see the piece I meant. Then her face got all nostalgic. "Oh," she said affectionately. "That's Molly's first bra."

"What?"

I hadn't even noticed Molly until she burst out with "What?" She was lying on a couch in the corner. (Old houses are neat, in many ways. How many houses have a couch in the kitchen?) Actually, it didn't surprise me that she was there. Molly's had the flu all of February, and she's kind of like a fixture, or a piece of furniture herself now, lying there with a box of Kleenex.

In a way, it's fun having Molly sick, because she's home all the time, instead of off with her friends after school and on weekends. We've been doing things we hadn't done since we were little, like playing Monopoly. It's fun to play with Molly, silly games like that, because she doesn't take them seriously. I build hotels all over everything, even on stupid old Baltic Avenue, and when she throws the dice and realizes she's going to land where I have hotels, she starts giggling. She moves her piece along, closer and closer, and laughs harder and harder till she gets there, and then sits him down, thump, by the hotel, and just starts counting out all her money. "You got me," she says. "I'm absolutely wiped out!" Then she hands over all her money, laughing, and says right away, "Let's play again."

I'm a terrible loser. I go around muttering "It

31

isn't fair" after I lose. I thought about it once, about what makes the difference, when I was feeling stupid and childish because I had cried after I lost a game of gin rummy, and said, "You cheated!" to Molly, even though I knew she hadn't. I think it's because Molly has always won at important things, or the things that are important to her, like making cheerleader, and having the best-looking boyfriend; so the little things, like Monopoly games, don't matter to her. Maybe someday, if I succeed at something, I'll stop saying "It isn't fair" about everything else.

It's also a nuisance, Molly being sick. She's grouchy, which isn't like her, because she's missing school—which means missing Tierney McGoldrick, even though he calls every day—and because she worries about how she looks. She can't be feeling *too* bad, because she spends a lot of time in front of the mirror in our room, trying to fix her hair which has gotten kind of scroungy looking, and putting rouge on her face, because it's so pale.

Sometimes, when Molly is messing around with a hairbrush and bobby pins, making herself even more beautiful, which isn't necessary, I kind of wish that she would notice *my* hair and offer to do something about *it*. I can't quite get up the nerve to ask her to. I'm almost positive she wouldn't laugh at me, but I can't bring myself to take the chance.

"Molly, don't get up," sighed Mom, because Molly was about to charge across the room to examine the piece of her bra. "Your nose will start up again."

Molly's flu consists mainly of nosebleeds. Mom says that's because she's an adolescent; Mom says that about almost everything. The doctor from the village says it's because of the cold weather, which damages the nasal membranes. Whichever it is, it's downright messy. Even though her side of our room is still nasty neat, the rug is spattered with Molly's dumb nosebleeds, which to my mind is a good deal more disgusting than anything I leave lying around on my side.

It was time for dinner anyway. Mom put the quilt away, which ended the argument they were about to have about the bra, and served pork chops and applesauce at the kitchen table. I had to move my salad plate over to the side to make room for Molly's box of Kleenex. Dad didn't say anything, even though he likes a tidy-looking table at dinner, because we've had a couple of unpleasant meals when Molly *didn't* bring her Kleenex.

It was a quiet meal, with Molly eating very carefully because of her nose, and Dad and I both a little preoccupied because it isn't all that easy to tuck something into your subconscious and keep it back there. Mom kept starting conversations that ended because nobody joined them. Finally she put down her fork, sighed, and said, "You know, much as I love this place, even in winter, I'll be glad when summer comes. You'll be feeling better about the book, Charles, because it'll be almost finished, and you girls can go to camp and you won't be so bored—"

"Camp," I said suddenly. *"Camp."* My mother stared at me. Molly and I have gone to the same camp every summer since I was eight and she was ten.

"Camp," said my father suddenly, looking at me with a grin starting.

"How much does camp cost?" I asked my mother.

She groaned good-naturedly. "Plenty," she said. "But don't worry about that all of a sudden. Your

33

father and I have always felt it was important enough that we've kept the money put aside each month. You girls will be able to go to camp."

"Mom," I said slowly, "do I *have* to go to camp?"

She was amazed. I've won the Best Camper Award for two years running for my age group. "Of course you don't have to go to camp, Meg. But I thought—"

"Lydia," announced my father. "I'm going to Boston tomorrow. I have to see my publisher, and I'm going to do some shopping. Meg and I are building a darkroom in the storeroom by the barn, if Will Banks doesn't mind. I'll call him tonight, Meg."

My mother was sitting there with a piece of lettuce on the end of her fork, shaking her head. She started to laugh. "This family is absolutely nuts," she said. "I haven't the slightest idea what anyone is talking about. Molly, your nose."

Molly grabbed a piece of Kleenex and clutched her nose. From behind her Kleenex she said haughtily, *"I* don'd know whad anyone is talking aboud either. Bud *I'm* going to camp, whether Meg does or nod."

Then she giggled. Even Molly realized how silly she looked and sounded, talking from behind a wad of tissues. "Thad is," she added, "if by dose ever stobs bleeding."

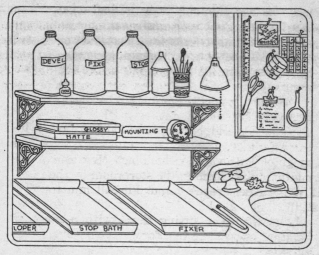

4

All of a sudden I know how Dad feels when he completes a chapter of the book. Or Mom, when one of her plants suddenly blossoms, or she finishes a new section of the quilt, and goes around with a smile on her face all day, even when no one's looking. I know how Molly must have felt when Tierney McGoldrick asked her to go steady, which is what happened two weeks ago. She came home wearing his tiny gold basketball on a chain around her neck, and was so giggly and cheerful and bounced around so much that Mom finally had to tell her to calm down so that her newly normal nose wouldn't have a relapse.

Molly's nose had finally stopped bleeding at the beginning of March, which is about the same time that the sun came out after a month of gray cold; Dr. Putnam in the village said that proved what he had thought, that the bad weather was causing her nosebleeds. Molly said she didn't care *what* caused them, she was just glad they were over, glad she could go back to school. Dad said he was sorry he hadn't bought stock in the Kleenex company.

I've hardly seen the sun at all because I've been in my darkroom. My darkroom! It's finished; it's all finished, and perfect. My father did it, just the way he said he would, and everything is just the way I dreamed of it. There is *nothing* that my father can't do.

The first pictures I developed were the ones of Will Banks. I'd had that roll of film tucked away in a drawer under my knee socks for almost two months. I was scared stiff when I developed it— scared that I had forgotten how, that I would do something wrong. But when I took the strip of negatives out of the tank and held it to the light, there were two pictures of the old house across the field, and then thirty-four pictures of Will, looking at me in thirty-four different ways. I felt like a genius, like an artist.

When the negatives were dry, I printed them all on one sheet. It's hard to see, from the negatives, exactly how a print will look, so I crossed my fingers again when I developed the contact sheet that would show me the real pictures for the first time. I stood there over the tray of developer and watched in the dim red light as the sheet changed from white to gray, and then saw the grays change to blacks and the shades become the faces of Will; after two minutes, there he was, looking up at me from the tray, thirty-four of him, still tiny, but complete.

When it was ready I took it, still dripping wet, into the kitchen and laid it on the counter beside the sink. Mom was there, peeling potatoes, and she looked over, first curiously, and then as if she were really surprised.

"That's Will Banks!" she said.

"Of *course* it's Will Banks," I told her, grinning. "Isn't he beautiful?"

She and I looked for a long time at all the tiny prints on the paper. There he was, lighting his pipe, and then smoking it, looking at me, half laughing. Then he leaned back in his chair—I had blown the focus on that one a little, when he leaned back, out of the range of focus. I should have realized that. But then there he was, sitting up straight, back in sharp focus again, looking at me with his eyes bright with interest; I remembered that he had been asking me questions about the camera, how I determined what settings to use. Toward the end of the roll, his eyes were looking past me and far off, as if he were thinking about something in the distance. He had been telling me about a camera that he had once, that he still had, if he could find it in the attic of the little house. He had bought it in Germany, he said, after the Second World War, when he was stationed there with the army. That surprised me.

"You were in the *army?*" I had asked him. The only people I knew who were in the army were boys who had flunked out of the university and didn't know what to do with themselves. Sometimes they would come back to see Dad in the house in town, with funny haircuts.

Will had laughed. "I was an officer," he said. "Would you believe it? People *saluted* me!" He put a stern look on his face and made a rigid salute. It was there, in the pictures.

Then he had laughed again, and puffed on his pipe. "In those days we all joined the army. It seemed important, then. For me, the best part was coming home. It was in summer, when I came

37

home, and Margaret had made ten blueberry pies, to celebrate. We ate blueberry pie for three days and then we were sick of blueberry pie and there were still six left over. I think she gave them away."

He had closed his eyes, remembering, still smiling. It was the last picture on the sheet. His eyes were closed, and the smoke from his pipe was a thin white line beside his head and circling across the top of the photograph.

I marked six of the tiny prints with a marking pen: my six favorites, each one a little different. Then I went back into the darkroom and spent the rest of the day enlarging those. I made two sets of them, so that I could give one of each to Will. I wondered if he'd be pleased. They were good pictures; I knew that, and both my parents had said so, too, and they never lie to me. But it must be a funny feeling, I think, to see your own face like that, caught by someone else, with all your feelings showing in it.

I took my own set of Will's pictures up to my room and taped them to the wall very neatly, with three above and three below. I've been trying to keep my half of the room neater ever since Molly drew the chalk line; every time my things start piling up and getting messy, Molly draws it over again, just to let me know it's still there.

She was on her bed, drawing pictures in her school notebook, when I went in and put the pictures on the wall.

"Mom'll kill you if you tear the wallpaper," she said, glancing over at me.

"I know it." We both knew it wasn't true. My Mother hardly ever gets mad. She scolds us sometimes, but the thought of Mom killing somebody is ridiculous. She doesn't even step on ants.

"Hey," said Molly suddenly, sitting up and

looking over at the wall. "Those are really *good.*"

I looked over to see if she was joking, and she wasn't. She was looking at Will's pictures with interest, and I could tell that she meant it, that she thought they were good.

"I like that one there, where he's looking off in the distance and smiling," she decided, pointing to one in the bottom row.

"He was talking about his wife," I remembered, looking at the photograph with her.

Molly sat there for a minute, thinking. She looked pretty again, now that she was feeling better. Her hair had gotten its curl back. "Wouldn't it be great," she said slowly, "to be married to someone who felt that way about you, so that he smiled like that whenever he thought of you?"

I hadn't ever really thought about it in such personal terms. To be honest, I find the whole idea of marriage intensely boring. But right at that moment I knew what Molly meant, and I could feel how important it was to her. "Tierney looks that way at you all the time," I told her.

"Really?"

"Sure. Sometimes when you don't even know he's looking at you. I saw him in assembly last Friday, looking over at you. Remember, you were sitting with the cheerleaders? He was watching you, and that's the way he looked, almost like Will is looking in the picture."

"*Really?*" Molly curled up on her bed and grinned. "I'm glad you told me that, Meg. Sometimes I don't know what's going on in Tierney's head at all. Sometimes it seems as if basketball is all he cares about."

"Well, he's only sixteen, Molly." All of a sudden I realized that I sounded like Mom, and I giggled. So did Molly.

"Hey, look Meg," she said, handing her notebook to me. "You're such a good artist, and I can't draw at all. Can you help me make these look better?"

She'd been drawing brides. Good old Molly. She's been drawing brides since she was five. Her drawing ability hadn't improved much in ten years, either, to tell the truth. But suddenly the idea of her drawing brides was kind of scary.

I took the ball-point pen. "Look," I told her. "Your proportions are all off. The arms are too short, even though you've tried to hide it with all those big bouquets of flowers. Just keep in mind that a woman's arms reach down to the middle of her thighs when she's standing up. Her elbows should reach her waist—look, your drawings all have elbows up by the bosom; that's why they look wrong. The necks are too long, too, but that's probably all right, because it makes them look glamorous. Fashion designers usually draw necks too long. If you look at the ads in Sunday's *New York Times,* you'll see—Molly?"

"What?"

"You're not thinking about getting *married?*"

Molly got huffy and took back her drawings. "Of course I'm thinking about getting married. Not now, stupid. But someday. Don't you think about it?"

I shook my head. "No, I guess I don't. I think about being a writer, or an artist, or a photographer. But I always think about myself alone, not with someone else. Do you think there's something wrong with me?" I meant the question seriously, but it was a hard question to ask, so I crossed my eyes and made a face when I asked it, and laughed.

"No," she said thoughtfully, ignoring my face-making, which was nice of her. "We're just different, I guess." She tucked the drawings into her notebook and put them on her desk very neatly, in line with her schoolbooks.

"Like you're pretty, and I'm not," I pointed out. What a dumb thing to say.

But I'll give Molly credit. She didn't try to pretend that it wasn't true. "You'll be pretty, Meg, when you get a little older," she said. "And I'm not sure it makes that much difference anyway, especially for you. Look at all the talent you have. And brains. I'm so *stupid*. What do I have, really, except curls and long eyelashes?"

I ruin everything. I should have known that she meant it sincerely. Molly is never intentionally snide. But she doesn't realize how it feels, for someone with stringy hair and astigmatism to hear something like that. How could she? I can't imagine how it would feel to be beautiful; how could Molly know how it feels *not* to be?

And I blew up, as usual. I struck a phony model's pose in front of the mirror and said sarcastically, "Oh, poor me, what do I have except curls and long eyelashes?"

She looked surprised, and hurt. Then embarrassed, and angry. Finally, because she didn't know what else to do, she picked up a pile of her school papers and threw them at me: a typical Molly gesture; even in anger, she does things that can't possibly hurt. The papers flew all over, and landed on my bed and the floor. She stood there a moment looking at the mess, and then said, "There, now you should feel right at home, with stuff all over so it looks like a pigpen." And she stormed out of the room, slamming the door, which was useless, because it fell open again.

I left the papers where they were, and Molly and I didn't talk to each other when we went to bed that night. Neither of us is very good at apologizing. Molly just waits a while after a fight, and then she smiles. Me, I wait until the other person smiles first. I always seem to be the first one in and the last one out of an argument. But that night neither of us was ready to call it quits, and Molly didn't even smile when I climbed into bed very carefully so that all her exercises in past participles stayed where she'd thrown them, and I went to sleep underneath the pile.

I don't know what time it was when something woke me up. I wasn't sure what it was, but something was happening that made me afraid; I had that feeling along the edge of my back, that cold feeling you get when things aren't right. And it wasn't a dream. I sat up in bed and looked around in the dark, shaking off whatever was left of sleep, and the feeling was still there, that something was very wrong. The French papers slid to the floor; I could hear the sound of them fluttering off the bed.

Quietly I got up and went to the window. The first day of spring wasn't very far away, but dates like that don't mean much in New England; it was still very cold, and there was snow, still, in the fields. I could see the whiteness of it as I looked out the window. Beyond the corner of the barn, far across, beyond the pine trees, there was a light in the window of the empty house. I looked up to find the moon, to see if it could be reflecting in one window, but there was no moon. The sky was cloudy and dark. But the light was there, a bright rectangle in one corner of the old house, and it was reflected in another rectangle on the snow.

"Molly," I whispered. Stupid to whisper, if you want to wake someone up.

But she answered, as if she were already awake. Her voice was strange. Frightened, and puzzled. "Meg," she said, in an odd voice, as if she were captured by something, as if she couldn't move. "Call Mom and Dad quick."

Ordinarily I argue with Molly if she tells me to do something, just on general principles. But everything felt wrong. She wasn't just telling me; she was ordering me, and she was very scared. I ran from the room, through the darkness, through the shadows in the hall, and woke my parents.

"Something's wrong," I told them. "Something's wrong with Molly."

Usually, when you turn a light on in the night, everything that you're afraid of goes away. At least that's what I thought once, when I was younger. Now I know it isn't true. When my father turned on the light in my bedroom, everything was there, it was so much there, and so bright, so horrible, that I turned and hid my face against the wall. And in the corner of the wall, with my face buried, my eyes closed tight and tears starting, I could still see it.

Molly was covered with blood. Her pillow, her hair, her face were all wet with it. Her eyes were open, frightened, and her hands were at her face, trying to stop it, trying to hold it back, but it was still coming, pouring from her nose onto the sheet and blanket in moving streams, and spattering on the wall behind her bed.

I could hear my parents moving very fast. I heard my mother go to the hall linen closet, and I knew she was getting towels. I could hear my father's low voice, talking to Molly very calmly, telling her everything was all right. My mother went to the phone in their bedroom, and I could hear her dial and talk. Then she moved down the stairs, and outside I heard the car start. "It's okay, it's okay," I heard my father say again and again, reassuring Molly in his steady voice. I could hear Molly choke and whimper.

43

Mom came back in the house and up the stairs, and came to where I was still standing with my back to the room. "Meg," she said, and I turned around. My father was in the doorway of the bedroom, with Molly in his arms like a small child. There were towels, already drenched with blood, around her face and head; they had wrapped her in the blanket from her bed, and the blood was moving on it slowly. My father was still talking to her, telling her it was all right, it was all right, it was all right.

"Meg," said my mother again. I nodded. "We have to take Molly to the hospital. Don't be scared. It's just another of those nosebleeds, but it's a bad one, as you can see. We have to hurry. Do you want to come with us?"

My father was moving down the stairs, carrying Molly. I shook my head. "I'll stay here," I said. My voice was shaking, and I felt as if I were going to be sick.

"Are you sure?" asked my mother. "We may be gone for quite a while. Do you want me to call Will and ask him to come up and stay with you?"

I shook my head again and my voice got a little better. "I'll be okay," I told her.

I could tell she wasn't sure, but my father was already in the car waiting for her. "Really, Mom, I'll be fine. Go on; I'll stay here."

She hugged me. "Meg, try not to worry. She'll be okay."

I nodded and walked with her to the stairs, and then she went down, and they were gone. I could hear the car driving very fast away from the house.

The only light on in the house was in my room, mine and Molly's, and I couldn't go back there. I walked to the doorway without looking inside, reached in and turned off the switch so that the whole house was dark. But the beginning of morning was coming; outside there was a very faint light in the sky. I took a blanket from my parents' bed, wrapped it around me, and went into my father's study, the little room that I had wanted to be mine. I curled up in his big comfortable chair, tucked the blue blanket around my bare feet, looked out the window, and began to cry.

If I hadn't fought with Molly this afternoon, none of this would have happened, I thought miserably, and knew that it wasn't true. If I had just said "I'm sorry" before we went to bed, it wouldn't have happened, I thought, and knew that that wasn't true, either. If we hadn't come here to live. If I'd kept my side of the room neater.

None of that makes any sense, I told myself.

The fields were slowly beginning to turn pink as the first streaks of sun came from behind the hills and colored the snow. It startled me that morning was coming; it seemed too soon. For the first time since I had heard Molly's frightened voice in our dark bedroom, I remembered the light in the old house. Had I really seen it? Now everything seemed unreal, as if it had all been a nightmare. On the far side of the pink fields the gray house was very dark against the gradually lightening sky, and its windows were silent and black, like the eyes of guardians.

But I knew that back in the blue-flowered bedroom the blood was still there, that it had not been a dream. I was alone in the house; my parents were gone, with Molly, with Molly's hair sticky from blood, and the stain spreading on the blanket around her. Those moments when I had stood shaking and terrified, with my eyes tightly closed against the corner of the wall, moments which may have been hours—I couldn't tell anymore— had really happened. I had seen the light in the

45

window across the fields, as well. I remembered standing and watching its reflection on the snow, and I knew it was real, too, though it didn't seem important anymore. I closed my eyes and fell asleep in my father's chair.

5

I made two Easter eggs, one for Will and one
for Molly. Not just plain old hard-boiled eggs that
you dye with those vinegar-smelling colors that
never come out looking the way you hoped they
would. Molly and I used to do that when we were
little—dozens of them, and then we wouldn't eat
them, and they turned rotten.

No, these were special, and there were only
two of them. I blew the insides out of two white
eggs, so that only the shells were left, very fragile
and light. Then I spent hours in my room, painting them.

Molly's was yellow, partly I guess because it
reminded me of her blond hair, and partly because
my parents told me that her hospital room was
depressingly gray-colored, and I thought that
yellow would cheer it up a bit. Then, over the pale

47

yellow egg, I used my tiniest brush and painted narrow, curving lines in gold, and between the lines, miniature blue flowers with gold and white centers. It took a long time, because the eggshell was so delicate and the painting so small and intricate; but it was worth it: when it was finished, the egg was truly beautiful. I varnished it to make it shiny and permanent, and when it was dry, I packed it in cotton in a box to protect it, and Mom took it with her when she drove to Portland to visit Molly. It worked, too; I mean it did make the room more cheerful, Mom said.

Molly was lots better, and coming home the next week. In the beginning she had been very sick. They had, first thing, given her blood transfusions; then, when she was feeling better, they decided to do a lot of tests to find out what was wrong, so that her nose wouldn't bleed anymore. They even had specialists see her.

You'd *think* that with medical science as advanced as it's supposed to be, that they could figure out what the trouble was and fix her up pretty quickly. I mean, *nosebleeds!* What's the big deal about that? It's not as if she had a mysterious tropical disease, or something.

But first, Mom said, after they put all that new blood into her, they started taking blood out, to test it. Then they did tests on the inside of her *bones*. Then they x-rayed her. Then, when they thought they knew what was causing the nosebloods, they started fooling around with all different kinds of medicines, to see what would work best. One day Mom and Dad went in, and when they came home, they told me that special medicine had been injected into Molly's spine. That gave me the creeps. It made me mad, too, because it seemed to me that they were just experimenting on her, for pete's sake. By that time they knew what the trouble

48

was—her blood didn't clot right—so they just should have given her whatever medicine would fix that and sent her home. But no, instead they started fooling around, trying different things, keeping her there longer.

And my parents were very strange about the whole thing. They were just like the doctors; they didn't even think of Molly as a person anymore. They talked about her as if she were a clinical specimen. They came home from the hospital and talked very coldly about different drugs with long names: whether this one was better than that one. They talked about reactions, side effects, contraindications; it was hard to believe they were talking about Molly.

I kept my mouth shut as long as I could. But then one night at dinner, the only thing they talked about was something called cyclophosphamide. There I was, sitting there with them, and I wanted to talk about other things: my darkroom, my Easter eggs that I was working so hard on, what I was going to do during spring vacation from school. *Anything.* Anything, that is, except cyclophosphamide, which I didn't know anything about and couldn't pronounce.

"Stop it!" I said angrily. "Stop talking about it! If you want to talk about Molly, then talk about *Molly,* not her stupid medicine! You haven't even sent in her camp application, Mom. It's still on your desk!"

They both looked as if I had thrown something at them. But it worked. I don't think I heard the word "cyclophosphamide" again, and for a while they talked of other things, and life was somewhat normal. And now Molly will be home soon, all better—and no more nosebleeds—and after all that business with the fancy drugs, it turned out that what she ended up with is pills.

When she comes home, she'll have to take pills for a while. Big deal. They could have found that out when she got there, and sent her home sooner.

But since they didn't, I made the Easter egg for Molly, to cheer her up, and I made another one for Will. Will's egg was blue, and special in a different way. I thought and thought about how to paint it, and finally I looked up spices in the encyclopedia, and found a picture of nutmeg. I painted tiny nutmeg blossoms all over his eggshell, intertwined so that they formed a complicated pattern of orange, brown, and green over the blue background. I varnished and packed it, and on Easter Sunday I took the box with his egg, and the envelope with his pictures, and walked down the road to his house.

I hadn't seen Will since Molly got sick. Things were just too complicated at first. My parents spent a lot of time at the hospital, and I had to do most of the cooking. Then, when she was getting better, my father had to work doubly hard on the book because he hadn't been able to concentrate on it when she was so sick. I realized that I hadn't been concentrating on my schoolwork, either, for the same reason, so I had a lot of catching up to do too.

But finally things were calming down. It was school vacation, Molly was getting better, and even the mud outside had dried up a little. At night it would still freeze, and in fact I noticed, as I walked past, that there were tire tracks frozen into the driveway of the big house across the field.

That was another reason I wanted to see Will. After that first awful night, when I had seen the light in the window, other things had been happening at the house. Nothing seemed as mysterious as that light in the middle of the night; still, I was curious. There was a car at the house occasionally, and the driveway had been cleared of the last spring-muddied bits of snow. Sometimes when the day was very quiet I could hear the sound of saws and hammers coming from the house. Once I had seen the figure of a man on the roof, working. It certainly looked as if someone were getting ready to move in. I asked my father if the nephew had gotten permission to turn the house into an inn, but Dad said he hadn't heard anything about it; on the other hand, Dad pointed out, he'd been so distracted and so busy that he probably wouldn't have noticed if spaceships had landed in the field.

Will was under the hood of his truck again. I should have taken my camera with me. If there is one way in which I will always remember Will, it is under the hood of that old truck.

"Is it your battery again, Will?" I called as I approached him.

He straightened up and grinned. "Meg! I was hoping someone would drop in for tea. In fact, I have the kettle on. I'm so glad fate sent you instead of Clarice Callaway. She's been hinting for years that she'll come to call someday, and I live in perpetual fear of seeing her heading down this road with her Sunday hat on and a fistful of overdue library slips to deliver."

I giggled. Clarice Callaway is the village librarian. She's eighty-two years old, and I'm not giving away any secrets when I say that, because she tells everyone that herself as soon as they're introduced to her. She's also the president of the Historical Preservation Society, and my father says that's a real exercise in irony, because Clarice herself is the best-preserved historical monument for miles around. Also, she has a crush on Will. He told me that whenever he goes to the library, she disappears into the ladies' room, and then comes out again with bright pink rouge on her cheeks, so that she looks like a French doll his sister had when she was a child.

He sighed and wiped his hands on a rag. "It's the radiator this time. In the winter it's the battery, and when spring comes it's the radiator. The tires go flat in summer. Sometimes I think I'll buy a new truck, but then I figure I'd have to learn to deal with a whole new set of disasters. At least now I *know* that every April the radiator hoses will break and the engine will overheat. Better to know what your enemy is before you confront him; right, Meg?"

"Right," I agreed, even though I wasn't at all sure I wanted to be confronted by enemies or disasters, whether I knew them or not.

"Come inside," Will said. "I have a surprise for you."

But my surprise was first. After Will had poured tea for both of us, I opened the big envelope and took out the pictures. I laid the six of them on the kitchen table and watched as Will picked them up one at a time. He didn't laugh or blush or say "Oh, I look *terrible*" the way kids do when they see pictures of themselves. I knew he wouldn't. He picked up each one and studied it, smiling at some, looking thoughtfully at others. Finally he chose the same one that was my favorite: the one where his eyes were closed, and the smoke from his pipe was a thin line along the side and the top of the photograph. He took it to the window and looked at it in better light.

"Meg," he said at last, "all of these are very, very good. You know that already, I'm sure. This is the best one, I think, because of the composition, and also because you hit on just the right combination of shutter speed and aperture setting. You see how the lines in the faces are perfectly sharp —you must have a pretty good lens on that little camera of yours—but you slowed it just enough so that the line of smoke has a slight blur to it, as it should. Smoke has an ephemeral quality, and you caught that, but you didn't sacrifice the clarity of the face. It's a *fine* photograph."

Why did I want to cry when he finished talking? I don't even know what ephemeral means. But something inside me welled up like hot fudge sauce —sweet, and warm, and so rich that you can't bear to have very much. It was because someone who was a real friend was having the exact same feelings I was having, about something that was more important to me than anything else. I bet there are people who go through a whole life and never experience that. I sat there with my hand around the warm mug of tea, and smiled at Will.

"Meg," he said suddenly, gulping his own tea. "I'll make a deal with you!"

I laughed. People say that to me at school, and it means that they want to copy my algebra homework, and in return I get the Hostess Twinkie from their lunch.

"Remember I told you that I had bought a camera in Germany?"

I nodded.

"It's a fine camera," Will said. "The best made, and of course something like that doesn't diminish with age. I don't know why I haven't used it in so long, except that I lost my enthusiasm for a lot of things when Margaret died. And that," he said gruffly, "is the last thing she would have wanted.

"But I'm going to get it out of the attic. The camera, and four lenses, and a set of filters that go with it. I want you to use it."

The hot fudge started up again. My own camera has just one lens, which can't be removed. I've read about using other kinds of lenses and filters, but I've never had a chance to try.

"I don't know what to say," I told him, and it was true. "What could I possibly do in return?"

"Oh, don't worry about *that!*" laughed Will. "I said I'd make a deal with you. I'm not going to let you off easily, either. In return, I want you to teach me to use the darkroom. Let me borrow your little camera while you're using mine, and we'll set up a regular schedule for lessons. I'll warn you that it's been a long time since I've undertaken to learn anything new. But my eyesight is good, and my hands are steady, still."

"But, Will," I wailed. "I'm only thirteen years old! I've never taught anybody anything!"

Will looked at me very sternly. "My dear Meg," he said, "Mozart wrote his first composition when he was five. Age is a meaningless commodity in most instances. Don't underrate yourself. Now is it a deal?"

I sat there for a moment, looking at my empty mug. Then I shook his hand. He was right; his hands were firm and strong and steady. "It's a deal, Will," I said.

I remembered the Easter egg. In a way it seemed almost silly, now, but I brought out the little box and gave it to him. He held the egg up gravely and examined the design; his eyes lit up with recognition.

"*Myristica fragrans,*" he pronounced solemnly. "Nutmeg. Am I right?"

I grinned at him and nodded. "I don't know about the mistica, or whatever you said, but it's nutmeg. You're right."

He put the egg into a shallow pewter bowl, and took it to the living room. After he had put the bowl on a small pine table by the window, both of us stood in the room and looked at it. The blue of the egg was the same muted blue as the oriental rug; the rust and green shades seemed to reflect the colors of the old wood and the hanging, well-tended plants. It was perfect there; Will didn't even have to say so. We just looked at it together as the April sunlight from the window fell onto the bowl and the fragile oval shell, outlined their shadows on the polished table, and then brightened a rectangle on the pattern of the carpet.

"Now, scoot," said Will. "I have to deal with my radiator."

I was just at the end of his muddy driveway, and his head was back under the hood of the truck, when I remembered. I turned and called to him.

"Will? I forgot to ask you about the big house!"

He brought his head out and groaned. "And I forgot to tell you my surprise!"

So I went back for a minute. I sat on the front steps and scratched Tip beside his ear, while Will pulled the radiator hoses off—"rotten old things," he said to them. "Why do you do this to me every spring?"—and told me about the house. My question, it turned out, was the same as his surprise.

"I was right here last month," he said, "with my head under the hood, as usual. The battery then, of course. And a car drove up with a young couple in it. They asked if I knew anything about that house.

"In the past year, at least ten people have asked me about the house, but they've always been the wrong people. Don't ask me how I know that. It's just something I can feel. And when this young couple—Ben and Maria, their names are—got out of their car, I could tell they were the right ones.

"Ben helped me clean the leads to the battery,

and Maria went in the kitchen and made tea for the three of us. By the time Ben and I had washed our hands and finished our tea, I had rented the house to them. When you know it's the right people, it's as easy as that.

"They don't have much money. He's a student still, at Harvard, and he said he was looking for a quiet place for the summer, to write his thesis."

I groaned. Next thing you knew, this whole valley would be noisy from the sound of typewriters. Will laughed; he'd had the same thought.

"But in return for the summer in the house, they're going to fix the place up. He's been working weekends ever since I told them they could have the house. The roof needs work; the wiring needs work; the plumbing needs work. Well, you know what it's like when you get old with no one to take care of you!"

We laughed together. I could tell already that I would like Ben and Maria, because Will did.

"And Maria's going to put in a garden when the ground thaws," he continued. "They'll be moving in officially quite soon, I think. And I've told them about you. They're looking forward to having you stop in, Meg."

Then Will looked a little sheepish, the first time I'd ever seen him look that way. "But I forgot to ask them something," he confessed.

"What?"

He looked in several other directions before he answered. He was embarrassed. Finally he explained, "I forgot to ask them if they're married."

I burst out laughing. "Oh, Will," I said, "do you think it matters?"

He looked as if it hadn't occurred to him that it might not matter. "Well," he said finally, "I can tell you that it would have mattered to *Margaret*.

But, well, I guess maybe you're right, Meg. I guess it doesn't really matter to me."

Then he wiped his hands on his rag and grinned. "It might matter to their child, though. From the looks of it, there's going to be a baby coming this summer."

A baby. That was a strange thing to think about. I'm not overly fond of babies. Molly adores them. She says she's going to have at least six someday herself, even though I keep telling her that's environmentally absurd.

I told Molly about it on the phone that night, and she was thrilled at the thought of having a baby in the house across the field. Her voice sounded good, stronger than it has since she got sick. I've talked to her on the phone a lot, and sometimes she's sounded tired and depressed. But now she's feeling well again, and she's looking forward to coming home.

"It's a drag, being here," she said. "Even though there are some good-looking doctors."

That made me laugh. I knew she was feeling normal again if she was noticing the doctors.

I told her how much Will liked his photographs, and that he was going to let me use his German camera.

"Hey, Meg?" she said. "Do me a favor?"

"Sure." Usually I wouldn't say "sure" without knowing what the favor was; but what the heck, she'd been pretty sick.

"Would you take my picture when I get home? I want a really good one, to give Tierney for his birthday this summer."

"Molly, I'll make you look like a movie star," I told her, and she giggled before she hung up.

6

Will Banks is learning to use the darkroom, and he's fantastic. Ben and Maria have moved into the house, and they're terrific. Molly is home, and she's being thoroughly unbearable.

Well, as they say, two out of three isn't bad.

I suppose you can't really blame Molly for being a pain. She was awfully sick; no one knows that better than I do. I don't think the sight of her lying there in all that blood will ever go out of my mind.

But apparently she got used to being the center of attention in the hospital. Who wouldn't, with all those specialists around? Still, here she is at home, and supposedly well—or why would they have discharged her from the hospital?—and she acts as if everyone should still be at her beck and call. And my parents put up with it; that's the amazing thing.

"Could I have a tuna fish sandwich?" asked Molly at lunchtime, the day after she came home. She was lying on the couch in the kitchen, in a pose like Playmate of the Month, except that she was wearing jeans and a sweatshirt.

"Do you want lettuce?" my mother asked her, scurrying to get the bread and mayonnaise. For pete's sake. Do you want lettuce. Two months ago she would have said, "Make it yourself, madam." That's what she would *still* say, to me.

And after all that, Molly didn't even eat the sandwich. She came to the table, ate two bites, and then drifted back to the couch and said she wasn't hungry after all.

"Are you sure you're feeling all right, dear?" asked Mom.

"Quit bugging me, will you?" said Molly, and she stormed off to our room, slammed the door (which fell open again; Molly will never learn that the door to our room is totally useless in a tantrum) and took a nap for the rest of the afternoon.

Molly never used to be like that. *I* used to be like that, sometimes, and I hated myself when I was. Now Molly is that way, and I find myself hating her, or at least hating what has happened to her to make her different.

My parents don't say a word. That's different, too. In the past, when one of us was grouchy, my mother always said and did things that were both understanding and funny, so that we would start to laugh and whatever was making us irritable would just disappear in a comfortable way. Or Dad would be very stern. He says he doesn't have time to waste on rudeness. "Shape up," he would

59

say. And we would shape up, because he didn't leave any choice.

But now Mom doesn't chuckle and tease when Molly is awful. Dad doesn't lay down the law. Instead, Mom gets worried and confused, which makes things worse. Dad gets tense and silent and goes off to his study without saying anything. It's as if an upsetting stranger has moved in with us, and no one knows what to do about it.

Part of why Molly is being so obnoxious, I think, is because she doesn't look very good, and it was always so important to Molly to look pretty. But she lost weight while she was in the hospital (because the food was so dreadful, she says), so that now her face is thinner than it used to be. And more pale. The paleness, I guess, is because she had to have the blood transfusions, and it probably takes the red blood cells a while to build up again.

Worst of all, for Molly, her hair is falling out. That's because of the pills she has to take, my parents said. One of the side effects is that your hair falls out! I told her that there might be medicines with *worse* side effects, like making your nose fall off, but no one thought that was very funny. My mother told her that when she is able to stop taking the medicine, after a while, her hair will grow back thicker and curlier than it was before, but when Mom said that, Molly just said, "Great," very sarcastically and kept staring at her comb full of blond strands. Then Mom said that if it got worse, they would buy her a wig, and Molly said, "Oh, *gross!*" and stomped off to our bedroom.

So things are kind of difficult at our house now. Molly can't go back to school until she gains a little weight and gets her color back. She says she won't go back to school *anyway* if her hair keeps falling out. Mom and Dad don't say much about school. They're depressed about the whole thing, I can tell.

It will just take time. If we're all patient and wait, everything will be the same as it used to be, I know.

Will Banks is very kind to Molly. He comes to the house three evenings a week to work in the darkroom, and he always brings something for her: a library book to read, or a candy bar, some little thing like that. One night he brought a handful of pussy willows that he had found behind his house: the first ones of spring, and Molly was thrilled. It was the first time I'd seen her really happy about something for a long time.

"Oh, Will," she said softly, "they're beautiful." She held them against her cheek and rubbed the softness like a kitten. We were sitting in the kitchen, and I took a small vase and ran some water into it.

"No water, Meg," said Will. "If you put pussy willows in water, they'll blossom and then die. Just put them in the vase alone, and they'll stay beautiful forever."

There's so much I don't know. I gave Molly the vase, without water, and she arranged the pussy willows in it; she took them up to our room and put them on the table beside her bed. That night, after we were in bed and Molly was already asleep, I looked over, and the moonlight was across the table and across Molly; behind her, on the wall, was the shadow of pussy willows.

It's not surprising that Will knows so much about so many things, because he has an incredible memory. When we began working together in the darkroom, I showed him, first, the basic procedures for developing film. I only showed him once. Then he did it himself, developing a roll that he had shot of his truck and his dog, using his own camera to make sure it was working properly before he gave it to me. He remembered everything: the temperatures, the proportions of chemicals, the timing right down to the second. His negatives were perfect. The pictures weren't great, because, as he said, he'd been "just fooling around, wanting to get the feel of the camera again," but they were technically perfect, developed exactly right.

And he's immensely curious. When I could see that he'd learned to develop film properly, I wanted to go on to the next step: printing the pictures. But Will said, "Wait. What would happen if, when I was developing the film, I purposely made the chemicals too warm? What would happen if I agitated them less? Or more? And what if I had underexposed the film, Meg, when I took the pictures? Couldn't I compensate for that when I developed the film, maybe by prolonging the developing time?"

I thought for a minute. Those things had never occurred to me, and they should have. Of *course* you could compensate.

"I never tried," I said, thinking. "But I bet you could. There must be a book that tells how. Let me—"

He interrupted me. He's also impatient, I've found, and very independent. "Oh, the heck with books, Meg. Let's figure it out for ourselves. Let's experiment. Someone must have figured it out once, in order to write a book. Why can't we do the same thing?"

So we did. That was a Monday night, and on Tuesday and Wednesday, each of us shot several rolls of film, purposely underexposing and overexposing them. On Wednesday night we developed them, each one a different way. We changed the temperatures on some, the developing time on some, the amount of agitation on some. And we did it! We figured out exactly how to compensate for all sorts of things, how to build up contrast, how to reduce it. We felt like a couple of miracle workers.

When we came out of the darkroom after three hours, Mom was in the kitchen, working on her quilt. She looked up and laughed. "You two sounded like a couple of crazy people in there," she said, "shouting at each other."

I giggled. We *had* been shouting. "Don't leave it in the developer so long, you moron!" I had shouted at Will. "You'll ruin it!"

"I'm *trying* to ruin it!" Will had bellowed back. "So I can figure out how to do it perfectly! How can you learn anything if you won't take risks?"

And *I* was supposed to be teaching *him*.

"Lydia," Will explained to Mom that night, sitting down to have a cup of tea before he went home, "genius disregards the boundaries of propriety. Genius is permitted to shout if shouting is productive."

Mom laughed again and snipped off the thread as she completed a red-and-white-striped square from a sunsuit I wore when I was three years old. She likes Will. "Well," she said, "I've been living with creative genius long enough that I should know that by now. Charles has been known to shout at his typewriter, if you can believe that."

Will nodded very seriously, chewing on the stem of his pipe. "Oh my, yes. It would be necessary to shout at one's typewriter now and then, I would think. Machinery needs that kind of discipline occasionally. Just today I was shouting at my truck radiator."

Mom was smiling as she measured off a new square in the quilt. It was good to see her relaxed

63

and smiling, the way she used to be, for a change. "How about your homework, Meg?" she asked. "You're not disregarding the boundaries of your homework too, are you?"

I groaned. But I'm keeping up with school, same as always. Suddenly, though, algebra and American history seem pretty dull compared to other things that are happening. I'll be glad when the term ends next month so that I can spend more time on photography. Molly will be completely well by then, too, and things will be easier. And I'll be able to see a lot of Ben and Maria.

Will took me to meet them just after they moved in. Molly came, too; I was surprised that she wanted to, because she's been so miserable and self-conscious about the way she looks that mostly she stays in our room. But when I asked her, she said what the heck, there wasn't anything better to do.

The three of us walked across the field on a hot, sunny Saturday afternoon that smelled like new growing things. We could have gone down the road, of course, but it seemed like the sort of day when walking across a field would be a nice thing to do. Wild flowers were just beginning to appear. They always take me by surprise. It seems, each year, as if winter will go on forever, even back in town. Then when you've resigned yourself to a whole lifetime of grayness, suddenly bright bursts of yellow and purple and white spring up in the fields, and you realize they've been hiding there all along, waiting.

Will was carrying a heavy stick that he sometimes uses when he's walking, especially in the rocky fields. He pointed here and there with the stick, at the little blossoms in the field and the shady border of the woods, as we walked along.

"*Anemonella thalictroides, Cerastium arvense,*

Cornus canadensis, Oakesia sessilifolia," he said. Molly and I glanced at him, grinning at each other, and didn't say anything.

"Uvularia perfoliata," Will went on, pointing with his stick to a light yellow, tiny, bell-shaped flower.

"Can you say that three times fast?" asked Molly, laughing.

"Yes," grinned Will back at her.

Suddenly I decided that he was really putting us on. "You're making all that up, Will!" I hooted. "You big phony! You had me fooled for a minute, too!"

He looked down his nose at me in a haughty sort of way, but his eyes were twinkling.

Then he pushed aside some underbrush with his stick, and pointed to a clump of small purple flowers. *"Viola pedata,"* he said, talking to Molly, ignoring me. "So called because the leaves resemble the foot of a bird. You believe me, don't you, Molly?"

Molly was laughing. The sun was shining through her thin hair, and for the first time since she'd been sick, there was color in her cheeks. "I don't know for sure, Will," she smiled. "I *think* I believe you, but the only wild flower I recognize is goldenrod."

He nodded. *"Solidago,"* he said. "Very common around here, a remarkable plant. But we won't see it bloom until the end of July. In the meantime, you should investigate some of these others, Molly. It would keep you busy until you can go back to school, and it would be good for you, being in the fresh air."

Molly shrugged. She didn't like being reminded of her problems. We walked on.

Ben and Maria were behind the house, starting a garden. They had a patch of ground dug up, and

65

Ben was standing in the middle of the turned earth, chopping at the lumps with a hoe. There was sweat all over his bare back—he wasn't wearing anything but faded, patched jeans—and even though there was a handkerchief tied around his head, his hair and beard were wet with sweat too. He smiled when he saw us.

"Ah, saviors!" he called. "You're coming to rescue me from this slave labor, right?"

"Wrong," called the girl who was sitting in the grass at the corner of the garden patch. "No rescue! I want to get my peas planted. Hi, Will!"

I burst out laughing. Will had told me very casually that there seemed to be a baby coming. That was the understatement of the year. Sometimes I forget that Will is seventy years old, and that he's a little shy about some things. Maria was so thoroughly pregnant that I thought we would do well to start boiling water immediately.

She was sitting with her legs crossed, and her middle was resting on her knees. She was wearing a man's shirt with the sleeves ripped out; her arms were bare and very tan, the same as her legs. The shirt was buttoned around her, but just barely; the middle button was pulled sideways by her stomach, and it was going to pop off very soon. I hoped she had a bigger shirt ready; either that, or that the baby would be born before long. It looked like it was going to be a race between the baby and the button, and I didn't know enough about either pregnancy or the art of mending to be able to predict which was going to detach itself first.

Maria had one long dark braid down her back, and a smile that included all three of us, as well as Ben, who was still leaning on his hoe.

"I'd like you to meet my two friends, Meg and Molly Chalmers," Will said. "Meg is the photogra-

66

pher I've been telling you about. And Molly is the cheerleader, but I'm going to try to turn her into a botanist. Girls, this is Ben Brady. And Maria."

Maria reached up to shake our hands, and said, "Maria Abbott." Out of the corner of my eye I could see Will flinch slightly. It all went right over Molly's head. She was so interested in the baby.

"When is the baby due?" asked Molly. "Do you mind my asking? I just love babies."

From the garden, where he had started to hack at a clod of earth that obviously had a rock in the middle of it, Ben looked up and chuckled. He rolled his eyes. "Does she *mind* your asking? Prepare yourself, Molly, for an hour . . . two hours, *three* hours . . . of conversation. That's all she talks about! I remember a time—it wasn't so long ago, either, come to think of it—when Maria and I used to talk about books. Music. The weather. Politics. Little things like that. Now we sit down in the evening after supper, and we pour a couple cups of tea, put some Beethoven on the stereo, and talk about diapers." He groaned, but he was looking at Maria affectionately.

We were all laughing, even Maria. She threw a handful of weeds at him lightly, and said, "Just hoe your row, Daddy. Molly, come in the house with me. I'll show you the cradle I've been refinishing."

She got to her feet awkwardly, and, standing, said, "Look!" She smoothed the shirt over her middle so we could see how round she was. "It isn't due until July. Can you believe that? It's incredible how big I am, but I'm sure July is right. Do you know how you figure out your due date? It's really easy. You add seven days to the date that your last period started, and—"

I started talking quickly to Will, because I could see how embarrassed he was by the conversation. Maria and Molly went in the house, and Ben put down the hoe. He showed Will and me how he had hauled rocks from the field to make a small wall beside the driveway, and the work he'd been doing on the roof. We wandered around for a long time, talking about what needed to be done to the old house; Will explained how things had been when he was a child, and Ben thought of how to make them that way again. We stood, finally, by a bare patch of earth beside the kitchen door, and Will described the flowers that had been there once, how his grandmother had emptied her dishwater there, over the flowers, and they had grown bigger and healthier than the other plants.

"Of course!" said Ben. "It probably had little scraped-off bits of food, organic stuff in it. She was mulching the flowers without even realizing it. That's cool; that's really cool. We should try that. I bet we could grow herbs there; Maria's dying to have an herb garden. 'Parsley, sage, rosemary, and thyme,' " he sang, off-key.

Will looked somewhat nonplused by Ben, Maria the whole thing. But he liked them; I could tell. And he was happy about the house; I could tell that, too.

Maria made iced tea for everyone, and we went inside. The house was furnished with odds and ends of things, most of them with the paint partly removed. Maria was busy refinishing everything. There was an old spinning wheel, and she said she was going to learn to spin. The cradle, which was almost finished. A rocking chair, partly done, with a pile of sandpaper on the seat. Ben's typewriter and books stood on a desk made from an old door balanced on two sawhorses. Will sat down in the only real chair, a big comfortable one with its stuffing popping out like milkweed from the pods in fall.

"Hope no one has hay fever," laughed Maria as Will sat down. "Every time anyone sits in that chair, feathers and dust fly all over the room. But I'm going to reupholster it after the baby's born."

Ben groaned. "She's gone mad, really mad," he teased. "I live in constant fear that some morning I'll wake up and find that she's sanded and scrubbed and peeled and painted me in the night!"

Maria leaned over and examined his bare foot. "Come to think of it," she mused, "that's not a bad idea. You could use a little work." Then she leaned her head for a moment against his blue-jeaned leg, and he rumpled the top of her hair with his hand.

I didn't say much. I was very happy, being there. The sun had gotten lower in the sky, and as it came through the windows it fell on Maria as she sat there on the floor leaning against Ben, in gold patterns on her shoulders and the thick braid of hair. I was making a photograph in my mind.

But Molly chattered on and on. It was good to hear her; all the tenseness and anger were gone. She and Ben and Maria talked about what the inside of the house needed: hanging plants in the sunny windows; fresh white paint on the old plaster walls; just the right kind of curtains. "I'll weave them myself!" Maria exclaimed; Ben sighed, smiled, and stroked her head.

On the way home, Molly lagged behind Will and me. She was gathering wild flowers, one of each kind. She said she'd press them, and Will told her he would help her to identify each one, that he had a book she could use.

"You know," I said slowly to Will, as we walked back through the field together, "I wish I were more like Molly. I mean, I wish I knew the right things to say to people. Sometimes I seem to just *sit* there."

"Meg," Will said, and he put his arm around me as we walked, "do you see that section of the woods over there, where the spruce tree is beside the birches?"

"Yes," I said, looking where he pointed.

"Not far into the woods, beyond the spruce, at the right time of year, there's a clump of fringed gentians. Have you ever seen a fringed gentian?"

How do you like that? When I said something really serious, really personal, for pete's sake, to my best friend, he wasn't even listening. He was still thinking about his plants.

"No," I told him, a little sarcastically. "I've never seen a fringed gentian."

"It will be after you've moved back to town," he said. "It won't bloom until the end of September, maybe even October. But I want you to come back, so I can show it to you."

"Okay," I sighed. I didn't care about his old fringed gentian.

"It's important, Meg," Will said. "You promise?"

Well, if it was important to him, all right. I would want to come back, anyway, and I didn't mind looking at his flower. Maybe he wanted to photograph it or something.

"I promise, Will," I said.

viola conspersa

7

Finally Molly has stopped being a grouch. It was gradual, and I'm not even sure the change is a good one. She hasn't gone back to being the old Molly she was before she was sick. She isn't giggly, funny Molly anymore, full of smiles and ideas and silly enthusiasm.

I don't know what she is, now. A stranger, mostly. It's as if she has become part of a different world. One that doesn't include me anymore, or even Mom and Dad. She's quieter, more serious, almost withdrawn. When I tell her about things that are happening at school, she listens, and asks questions, but it's as if she doesn't really care much; she's only listening to be polite.

Only a few things interest her now. She spends a lot of time with the flowers. In the past, for Molly, flowers were things to run through in a field, to pick, to bury your nose in, to arrange in a vase on the table. Now, with Will's help, she's learning about them; she reads the books he's brought to her, and identifies the wild flowers she's found in the fields. She classifies them, labels them, arranges them in order in a book that she's putting together. It takes most of her time. She's very careful, and very serious, about her flowers. We don't dare, ever, to tease her about them.

It's as if she has become, suddenly, old.

The other thing that still interests her is the baby. She visits Maria often, and they talk and talk about the baby. Molly is helping Maria to make clothes for it; they sew together, and when she finishes something, Molly smoothes it with such care, folds it neatly, and puts it away in the drawer they're filling with little things.

Even Ben and Maria seem a little puzzled by the concern Molly has for all those tiny nightgowns and sweaters. Once I heard Ben say to her, "Hey, Moll. It's *already* going to be the best-dressed kid in the valley. Quit sewing for a while, will you? Come with me to see if we can find some wild strawberries."

But Molly just smiled at him and shook her head. "You go ahead, Ben," she said. "Take Meg. I want to finish this. I want everything to be perfect when the baby comes."

Ben groaned. "Molly, don't you *know* what babies are like? It's just going to pee on those clothes. Why do you need to be perfect with that kind of future in store for them?"

Molly smiled at him and went on stitching.

And sometimes, for no reason, Molly is like a baby, herself. One night after supper, when it was raining outside, we were sitting in front of the fireplace. Mom was working on the quilt, Dad was reading, and Molly and I were just watching

72

the logs shift and send sparks into the chimney as they burned. We had our pajamas on.

Suddenly, very quietly, Molly got up, went over to Dad, and climbed onto his lap. He didn't say anything. He just put his book down, put his arms around her, held her, and watched the fire. She put her head on his shoulder like a sleepy two-year-old, and with one hand he stroked the fine, wispy, babylike hair she had left.

I could understand, I guess, the change in Molly if she were still sick. But she isn't; she's perfectly well. She is still taking the pills, and every few weeks Mom takes her to Portland to the hospital, for tests, to make sure everything is okay. Soon, the doctors said, she'll be able to stop taking the pills altogether, and then her hair will grow back. She'll win a beauty contest, the specialist told her, when she has her curls again.

Mom told us that at dinner, after they had come back from the hospital, and Molly just smiled, the casual and tolerant kind of smile that most people give to small children who say foolish things. But there was a time when it would have meant something to Molly, to be told she was beautiful.

Well, things change. I just have to learn to adjust to what they change to.

One morning early in June, my father came into the kitchen, poured himself a cup of coffee, and sighed. I was just finishing my breakfast and had planned to spend all of Saturday morning in the darkroom. I had photographed Maria by her kitchen window, and Will and I were experimenting with different kinds of paper for the finished prints. I could hardly wait to try printing Maria in different contrasts, textures, and tones.

But when Dad pours a cup of coffee, sits down in the kitchen and sighs, I know I'd better stick around because something's up.

"I just got a phone call," he said, "from Clarice Callaway."

"Are your books overdue?" I asked. "She's a real stickler about overdue books."

He laughed. "No, she and I have achieved a pretty good understanding about my overdue books. I wish that's all it were. She started the conversation by saying, 'I don't want to meddle, but—' You know what that means."

"It means she wants to meddle. Sometimes she starts with, 'I don't mean to be inquisitive, but—.' "

"Right. And that means she means to be inquisitive. I can see you have Clarice figured out, Meg. Well, this time she's upset about Will renting the house. She says the whole village is up in arms—which I assume is a Callaway exaggeration—because there are hippies living in Will's house."

"Hippies? What's that supposed to mean?"

Dad frowned. "*I* don't know. Ben has a beard, and I guess by Clarice's definition that makes him a hippie. But maybe you can shed some light on the things she brought up. Is it true that Ben and Maria are growing marijuana behind the house?"

I started to laugh. "Dad, of course not. They've put in peas and strawberries so far. Ben wants to plant squash, but he hasn't decided what varieties yet. And his tomatoes and beans go in this week."

"Is it true that they walk around nude?"

"Good grief, Dad. No, it isn't true, but even if it were, whose business would it be? They're out in the middle of nowhere. One afternoon Maria took off her shirt and lay in the sun. When I came along, she had her shirt off, and she asked me if I minded. I said I didn't, and she left it off for a

74

while. She gets so hot and uncomfortable, because the baby's due soon."

"Well, that was another of Clarice's topics. Is it true that they're planning to have that baby by themselves, in the house?"

"Yes. But they've both been reading everything they can find about delivering a baby. Maria's doing all sorts of exercises, and they took a course together in Boston. And Dr. Putnam in the village has agreed to come if they need him."

Dad scratched his head. "No chance that they'll change their minds about that?"

"I don't think so, Dad. It's very important to them. They're really excited about doing it themselves, about having the baby born there in the house, instead of in a hospital. They don't like the impersonal qualities of a hospital. But the baby's important to them, too. They're doing everything they can to be sure the baby will be safe and healthy."

"Well, I guess I can try to convince Clarice of that. So that leaves only one thing. They *are* married, aren't they?"

I stirred the last soggy Rice Krispies in the bottom of my bowl. "They love each other. They talk about being old together, sitting in rocking chairs on their porch, and what it will feel like to kiss each other when they have false teeth and bifocals."

"That's not what I asked. Are they married?"

Funny how Rice Krispies stick to a bowl when they're wet. I really had to pry them loose from the sides of the bowl with my spoon. "I don't think so, Dad. Maria doesn't wear a wedding ring, and her last name is different from Ben's."

My father winced. "That's what I was afraid of. I don't quite know how to deal with that one. And Clarice has already called Will's nephew in

Boston. Well, maybe you should talk to Ben and Maria about it, Meg. They might as well be prepared."

Great. What was I supposed to do, go tell my friends who were going to have a baby next month that I thought they ought to get married? What business was it of mine?

Still, my father was right. They ought to know what was going on. I gave up my plans for working in the darkroom that morning. Ben and Maria had asked if they could see some of my photographs, so I took the ones I'd done of Will, and two that I'd just finished of Molly. She hadn't even noticed my taking them; she'd been sitting on the front steps, working on some of her wild flowers. With Will's help, she'd mounted each of the flowers she'd pressed, and labeled them with their Latin names. One of the pictures showed Molly holding a blossom of Queen Anne's lace up against the sunlight; both she and the blossom were in silhouette. The other photograph was of her bent head, with what was left of her curly hair falling down over her face as she arranged some tiny flowers on a page.

Ben and Maria were hanging sheets and towels on the clothesline behind their house when I got there. They did their wash together every Saturday, using an old wringer machine that they'd bought at a garage sale. Ben always teased Maria that if she didn't have the baby on time, he would put her through the wringer and squeeze it out; just thinking about it makes my stomach lurch, but Maria thought it was funny.

"Hey, Meg!" Ben called cheerfully when he saw me coming. "This time next month, we'll be hanging diapers!"

"You mean *you'll* be hanging diapers," laughed Maria, as she snapped a wet dish towel into the

76

air to get the wrinkles out. *"I'm* going to be lying in bed, being waited on. Having tea brought to me on a tray, while I recover!"

Knowing Maria, I didn't think she was going to be spending much time in bed recovering. She'd probably be up and around the day after the baby arrived, sanding the floors, building a bookcase, making raspberry jam. I talked her into letting me help Ben with the rest of the laundry, and she went inside to make a pot of tea.

We sat around their little painted kitchen table and shared tea with fresh mint in it. I took out the photographs to show them. They loved the ones of Will, because they love Will. But the two of Molly were better. They thought that, and I could see the difference, too. Partly it was because I have been learning so much from working with Will; partly it was because I was using his German camera now. He had taught me to use the different lenses; I had shot these two of Molly with the 90mm lens, and I'd been able, that way, to do it from a distance, so that she hadn't known I was doing it. The look on her face was absorbed, preoccupied with her flowers; the fine lens caught the sharp outline of sunlight on her hair and the shadows across her face and hands.

"I asked Molly if she wanted to come with me this morning," I explained, "but she wasn't feeling well. She said to say hi, though, and to see how you're coming with the cradle."

Maria grinned with pride and pointed into the living room, where the cradle stood, finished. It glowed with wax; folded over one side was a soft yellow crocheted blanket.

"Meg," asked Ben hesitantly, "what's wrong with Molly?"

I told them about her illness, about the nosebleeds, the hospital, the transfusions, and the pills

77

that were making her hair fall out. They were both very quiet. Ben reached over and ran his hand gently over the top of my head. "That's rough," he said. "That's very rough."

"Well," I explained, "it's not that big a deal. And she's lots better. Look." I pointed to one of the photographs. "See how round her face is getting? She's gained ten pounds since she came home from the hospital."

Maria poured more tea into our cups. "I'm glad we came here, Ben," she said suddenly, "for Molly. She's so excited about the baby."

That reminded me why I had come to see them. "Ben? Maria?" I said. "You know the little church in the village?"

"Sure," Ben said. "The white steeple. It looks like a postcard picture. Why? You going to photograph it?"

"No," I said. "But last Saturday, when I was in town with Mom to buy groceries, there was a wedding there. It was really neat. The bride came out and threw her bouquet from the step. The bridesmaids all had light blue dresses on, and—" I hesitated. "Well, I don't know. It was just nice."

Ben and Maria were both making faces. Ben is quite good at making faces; he screwed his mouth up sideways and crossed his eyes. "Weddings," he said. "Yuck."

Maria rolled her eyes and agreed with him. "Yuck," she said.

"*Why?*" I asked. "What's wrong with getting married, darn it?"

They both looked surprised. "Nothing's wrong with getting *married*," Ben said. "It's weddings that are so awful. What do you think, Maria, shall we show her?"

Maria grinned and nodded. "Yeah," she said. "She's a good kid."

Ben went into the living room and took a box out of the closet. He brought it back to the kitchen table and set it down. He leered, fingered his beard, and said in a diabolical voice. "Ya wanna see some feelthy pictures, lady?" Then he opened the box.

I started to laugh. They weren't bad photographs; in fact, technically, they were very good photographs, even though I'm not crazy about color.

But they were *awful*. And they were of Ben and Maria's wedding, for pete's sake. They were in a thick white leather album that said *Our Wedding* on the cover in gold letters. And I could see, while I looked at them, what Ben and Maria meant about yucky weddings.

There were the tuxedos, and the tails, and the top hats. There was Maria with her dress pulled up to show a lacy blue garter. There were the huge baskets of flowers beside the altar of the church. "Know what happened to those flowers?" Maria asked. "Two hundred dollars' worth of flowers? They got thrown away as soon as the service was over."

There was the wedding cake, about three feet high, decorated with birds and flowers and frosting ribbons. "Know how much that cake cost?" grinned Ben. "A hundred bucks. Know what it tasted like? Cardboard."

There were hundreds of people drinking champagne. "Know who those people are?" asked Maria. "My parents' friends. Ben's parents' friends. Know what they're doing? Getting drunk, on five hundred dollars' worth of champagne."

And there were Ben and Maria, surrounded by people, flowers, food. They were smiling at the camera, but they both looked as if they didn't mean it much.

79

"Know who that is?" Ben asked. I nodded. "That's Ben Brady and Maria Abbot, who wanted to get married in a field full of daisies beside a stream. Who wanted to have guitar music instead of a five-piece band; homemade wine instead of champagne," he said. He slammed the book closed and put it back in the box.

"Why didn't you?" I asked.

They shrugged. "Oh, sometimes it's just easier to please people," Maria said finally. "Ben's parents wanted a big wedding. My parents wanted a big wedding. We did it for them, I guess."

"Can I ask you a funny question?"

"Sure."

"Why don't you both have the same last name?"

It was Maria who answered me. "You know, Meg, I had the name Abbott all my life. Maria Abbott did things that I was proud of. I won a music award in high school, and I was Maria Abbott. I was elected to Phi Beta Kappa in college, something I worked hard for, and I was Maria Abbott. When I realized I wanted to marry Ben, I also realized that I didn't want to stop being Maria Abbott. Ben could understand that. There's no law that says a wife must take her husband's name. So I didn't. Someday you may feel the same way about Meg Chalmers."

Right now I know there's no one I would rather be than Meg Chalmers. It's a funny thing about names, how they become part of someone. I thought suddenly of the little boy Will Banks, years ago, who sat in a room angry and sad, and carved WILLIAM on the closet floor.

"Hey," I said, Funny I hadn't thought to ask before. "The baby. What are you going to name him? Her? It?"

Maria groaned. "Ask any other question, Meg. *Don't* ask what we're going to name him her

80

it. We can't decide. We fight about it all the time. We scream at each other. It's *awful*."

Ben said, "I've quit worrying about it. I figure the baby is going to arrive and before it does anything else, it's going to shake hands all around and say, 'Hi. I'm — — —.' " That's the only way we're going to know what its name is."

Then he jumped up, bounded through the living room, and opened a door. "But look! This is where it will be born!" I looked through the living room and saw an empty room beyond, very clean, its walls freshly painted white, with a brass bed alone in the center.

"And this is where it will sleep," said Maria, smiling, touching the cradle with her bare foot, so that it rocked slightly.

"And this is what it'll wear!" said Ben proudly, reaching into the drawer of a partly sanded pine chest, and pulling out a tiny blue nightgown. The drawer was filled with little folded things.

"This is what it'll eat!" grinned Maria, cupping her hands around her breasts.

"And—" Ben stood still suddenly, in the middle of the living room. "Meg, come. I want to show you something." He took my hand, and I followed him out the back door, picking up my photographs on the way. It was almost lunchtime.

Ben took me past the garden where the peas were thriving against the wire trellises, across the newly cleared space where he'd been pulling up alders, past the little wooden bird feeder that Maria filled with seeds each morning. Behind a clump of young pine trees, he had pulled out brush and exposed part of a rock wall that had been there, I knew, for more than a hundred years. The sunlight filtered down through the nearby woods into the little secluded space; he had cut the grass there, and it was very soft, very green, very quiet.

He put his arm over my shoulders and said, "This is where we'll bury the baby, if it doesn't live."

I couldn't believe it. I pushed his arm off me and said, *"What?"*

"You know," he said firmly, "sometimes things don't work out the way you want them to. If the baby dies, Maria and I will bury it here."

"It's not going to die! What a horrible thing to say!"

"Look, Meg," Ben said, "you can *pretend* that bad things will never happen. But life's a lot easier if you realize and admit that sometimes they do. Of course the baby's probably going to be just fine. But Maria and I talked about the other possibility, too. Just in case; just in case."

I turned away from him and left him standing there. I was so angry I was shaking. I looked back; his hands were in his pockets, and he was watching me.

I said, "Just in case you're interested, Ben Brady, I think you're an absolutely rotten person. That baby doesn't deserve you for a father."

Then I walked home, and on the way home I was sorry I had said it, but it was too late to go back.

8

Molly is in the hospital again, and it's my fault.

Why can't I learn when to keep my mouth shut? I'd already said something I regretted, to Ben, and hadn't had the nerve to go to him and apologize. It was just a week later that I blew it with Molly.

She was lying on her bed, in her nightgown, even though it was eleven in the morning. She's gotten so darn lazy, and my parents don't even say anything to her about it. That's partly why I was mad at her, to begin with, because she was still in her nightgown at eleven in the morning.

She was grouchy and mad, too. I'm not sure why. I think mostly it was because school had just ended, before she'd even had a chance to go back. Tierney McGoldrick hardly ever calls her anymore. She doesn't know it, but toward the end of school he started dating a red-haired senior girl. At least I was smart enough not to tell Molly *that*.

But there she was, lying on her bed, grumbling about how awful she looks. I am so sick of hearing Molly talk about how she looks. Her face is too fat. Her hair is too thin. To hear her talk, you'd think she was really a mess, when the truth is that she's still a billion times prettier than I am, which is why I'm sick of listening to her.

I told her to shut up.

She told me to drop dead, and before I dropped dead, to pick up my sneakers from her side of the room.

I told her to pick them up herself.

She started to get up, I think to pick up my sneakers and throw them at me, and when she swung her legs over the side of the bed, I suddenly saw what they looked like.

"Molly!" I said, forgetting about the sneakers. "What's wrong with your *legs?*"

"What do you *mean*, what's wrong with my legs?" No one had ever criticized Molly's legs before; in fact, even I have to admit that Molly's got nice legs. She held up her nightgown and looked down.

Both of her legs were covered with dark red spots. It looked like a lot of mosquito bites, except that they weren't swollen.

"Does it hurt?"

"No," she said slowly, looking puzzled. "What could it be? It wasn't there yesterday; I know it wasn't."

"Well, it's there now, and it sure looks weird."

She pulled her nightgown down to cover her legs. Then she got into bed and pulled the covers up around her. "Don't tell anyone," she said.

"I will, too. I'm telling Mom." I started out of the room.

"Don't you *dare*," Molly ordered.

I'll be darned if I'll take orders from Molly. Anyway, I really thought my parents ought to know. I went downstairs and told Mom that there was something wrong with Molly's legs; she jumped up with a frightened look and went upstairs. I stayed out of it after that, but I listened.

I heard Mom and Molly arguing. I heard my mother get my father from the study. Then more arguing with Molly. I heard my mother go to the upstairs phone, make a call, and go back to Molly.

Then Molly crying. Yelling. I had never in my life heard Molly like that before. She was screaming, "No! I won't! I won't!"

Things quieted after a few minutes, and then my father came down. His face was very drawn, very tired. "We have to take Molly back to the hospital," he told me abruptly, and without waiting for me to answer, he went out to start the car.

Mom came downstairs with Molly. She was in her bathrobe and slippers, and she was sobbing. When they were by the front door, Molly saw me standing all alone in the living room. She turned to me, still crying, and said, "I hate you! I hate you!"

"Molly," I whispered, "please don't."

They were in the car and ready to leave when I heard my mother call to me. I went outside, letting the screen door bang behind me, and walked over to the car. "Molly wants to tell you something," Mom said.

Molly was in the back seat, huddled in the corner, rubbing her eyes with the back of her hand. "Meg," she said, choking a little because she was trying to stop crying, "tell Ben and Maria not to have the baby until I get home!"

"Okay," I nodded. "I'll tell them." As if they had any control over it! But I would tell them what Molly said, just because Molly asked me to. At that point I would have done anything in the world for Molly.

I went back upstairs, picked up my sneakers and put them in the closet. I made Molly's bed. The pussy willows were still there, in their little vase. The photographs of Will were back on the wall, and the two of Molly and her flowers were with them now. The chalk mark was still there, faded, but there. It was a nice room, except that an hour before, Molly had been in it, and now she wasn't, and it was my fault.

I went down to the darkroom, gathered up the photographs of Maria I'd been working on, and walked across the field to their house.

Will Banks was there, having lunch with Ben and Maria. They were all sitting outside at the picnic table, eating the entire crop of peas. There was a huge bowl of them in the middle of the table, and they were each eating from it with their own spoons, as if it were the most normal sort of lunch in the world.

"Hey, Meg!" Ben greeted me. "How's it going? Have a pea. Have *two* peas!"

He fed me two peas from his spoon; they were the tenderest, sweetest peas I've ever eaten. I sat down on the bench beside Will, and said, "Molly's back in the hospital, and she says please don't have the baby until she comes home. I know that's a dumb thing to say," and then I started to cry.

Will Banks put his arms around me and rocked me back and forth as if I were a baby. I cried until his shirt collar was wet clear through, saying "It's my fault, it's my fault, it's my fault" over and over again. Will said nothing except "There. There."

Finally I stopped crying, sat up straight, blew

my nose on the handkerchief Will gave me, and told them what had happened. No one said very much. They told me, of course, that it wasn't my fault. I knew that already. Ben said, "You know, sometimes it's nice just to have someone to blame, even if it has to be yourself, even if it doesn't make sense."

We sat there quietly for a minute, and then I asked if I could borrow Maria's spoon. She wiped it on her napkin and gave it to me, and I ate all the peas that were left in the big bowl. There were *pounds* of peas, and I ate them all. I have never been so hungry in my life.

The three of them watched in amazement while I ate all those peas. When I was finished, Maria started to giggle. Then we all started to laugh, and laughed until we were exhausted.

It is so good to have friends who understand how there is a time for crying and a time for laughing, and that sometimes the two are very close together.

I took out the photographs of Maria. Will had seen them, of course, because we'd worked on them together. He is as able in the darkroom now as I am, but our interests are different. He is fascinated by the technical aspects of photography: by the chemicals, and the inner workings of cameras. I don't care so much about those things. I care about the expressions on people's faces, the way the light falls onto them, and the way the shadows are in soft patterns and contrast.

We looked at the pictures together, and talked about them. Ben was much like Will, interested in the problems of exposure and film latitude; Maria was like me: she liked seeing how the shadows curved around the fullness of the baby inside her, how her hands rested on the roundness of her middle, how her eyes were both serene and excited at the same time.

"Meg," she said, "Ben and I were talking about something the other night, and we want you to think it over and talk about it with your parents. If you want to, and if they don't mind, we'd like you to photograph the birth of the baby."

I was floored. "Golly," I said slowly, "I don't know. It never occurred to me. I mean, I don't want to intrude."

But they were both shaking their heads. "No," Ben said. "It wouldn't be an intrusion. We wouldn't want just anyone there, and of course you'd have to be careful to stay out of the way and not to touch anything sterile. But you're special, Meg; you're close to us. Someday Maria and I would like to be able to look back at that moment. We'd like the baby, someday, to be able to see it, too. You're the one who can do it, if you want to."

I wanted to, desperately. But I had to be honest with them, also. "I've never seen a baby being born," I said. "I don't even know much about it."

"Neither have we!" Maria laughed. "But we'll prepare you for that part. Ben will show you our books, and explain everything in advance so that you'll know exactly what to expect when the time comes. Only, Ben," she added to him, "I think you'd better do it *soon*, because I don't know how much longer we have. The calendar says two weeks, but there are times when I wonder if it might be sooner."

I promised to talk to my parents, and Ben said he would, too. Suddenly I thought of something. "What if it's born at night?" I asked. "There won't be enough light. I could use a flash, I suppose, but—"

Ben held up one hand. "Don't worry!" he said. He cupped his hands into a megaphone and held them against Maria's stomach. Then he spoke to the baby through his hands: "Now hear this, kid. You are under instructions to wait until Molly comes home. Then come, but do it in daylight, you hear?

"That'll do it," Ben said. "Maria and I are determined to have an obedient child."

Before I left, I took Ben aside and spoke to him alone. "I'm sorry, Ben, for what I said that day."

He squeezed my shoulders. "That's okay, Meg. We all say things we're sorry for. But do you understand now what I was talking about that day?"

I shook my head and answered him seriously, honestly. "No. I think you're wrong, to anticipate bad things. And I don't understand why you even want to think about something like that. But I'm still sorry for what I said."

"Well," Ben said, "we're friends, anyway. Hang in there, Meg." And he shook my hand.

Will walked me home across the field. He was very quiet. Halfway home, he said, "Meg, you're very young. Do you think it's a good idea, really, being there when that child is born?"

"Why not?"

"It might be very frightening. Birth isn't an easy thing, you know."

"I know that." I dislodged a small rock with one toe and kicked it through a clump of tall grass. "For pete's sake, Will, how can I learn if I don't take risks? You're the one who taught me that!"

Will stopped short and thought for a minute. "You're absolutely right, Meg. Absolutely right." He looked a little sheepish.

I looked around the field. "Will, what happened to all those little yellow flowers that were here last month?"

"Gone until next June," he told me. "They've all

been replaced by July's flowers. Molly's goldenrod will be in bloom before long."

"I *liked* those little yellow ones," I said grumpily.

" 'Margaret, are you grieving over Goldengrove unleaving?' " Will asked.

"What?" I was puzzled. He never called me Margaret; what was he talking about?

He smiled. "It's a poem by Hopkins. Your father would know. 'It is the blight man was born for, It is Margaret you mourn for,' " he went on.

"Not me," I told him arrogantly. "I *never* mourn for myself."

"We all do, Meg," Will said. "We all do."

That was three weeks ago. July is almost over. Molly isn't home yet. The baby hasn't been born, so I suppose it's following Ben's instructions and waiting for her. I've studied the books on delivering babies with Maria and Ben, and I'm ready to do the photographs. My parents don't mind. When I asked them, they said "Sure" without even discussing it. They're very preoccupied. I know why, finally.

It was a few nights ago, after supper. My dad was smoking his pipe at the kitchen table. The dishes were done; Mom was sewing on the quilt, which is almost finished. I was just hanging around, talking too much, trying to make up for the quiet that had been consuming our house. I even turned the radio on; there was some rock music playing.

"Hey, Dad, dance with me!" I said, pulling at his arm. It was something silly we used to do sometimes, back in town. My dad is a *terrible* dancer, but sometimes he used to dance with Molly and me in the kitchen; it used to break my mother up.

He finally put down his pipe and got up and started dancing. Poor Dad; he hadn't gotten any better since the last time we did it, and I think I have, a little. But he's pretty uninhibited, and he tried. It was dark outside; we had eaten late. Mom turned on the light, and I could see on the kitchen walls some of the drawings of wild flowers that Molly had been doing, that she had hung here and there. Dad and I danced and danced until he was sweating and laughing. Mom was laughing, too.

Then the music changed, to a slow piece. Dad breathed a great sigh of relief and said, "Ah, my tempo. May I have the pleasure, my dear?" He held out his arms to me and I curled up inside them. We waltzed slowly around the kitchen like people in an old movie until the music ended. We stood facing each other at the end, and I said suddenly, "I wish Molly was here."

My mother made a small noise, and when I looked over at her, she was crying. I looked back at Dad in bewilderment, and there were tears on his face, too, the first time I had ever seen my father cry.

I reached out my arms to him, and we both held out our arms to Mom. She moved into them, and as the music started again, another slow, melancholy song from some past summer I couldn't remember, the three of us danced together. The wild flowers on the wall moved in a gradual blur through our circling and through my own tears. I held my arms tight around the two of them as we moved around in a kind of rhythm that kept us close, in an enclosure made of ourselves that kept the rest of the world away, as we danced and wept at the same time. I knew then what they hadn't wanted to tell me, and they knew that I knew, that Molly wouldn't be coming home again, that Molly was going to die.

9

I dream of Molly again and again.

Sometimes they are short, sunshine-filled dreams in which she and I are running side by side in a field filled with goldenrod. She's the old Molly, the Molly I knew all my life, the Molly with long blond curls and her light laugh. The Molly who runs with strong tan legs and bare feet. She runs faster than I can, in my dream, looks back at me, laughing, and I call to her, "Wait! Wait for me, Molly!"

She holds out her hand to me, and calls, with her hair blowing around her, streaked with sun, "Come on, Meg! You can catch up if you try!"

I wake up; the room is dark, and her bed is empty beside mine. I think of her somewhere in a hospital I have never seen, and wonder if she is dreaming the same dream.

Sometimes they are darker dreams of the same field. I am the one, in this darker dream, who has run faster; I have reached some misty destination, a dark and empty house, where I stand waiting for her, watching her from a window as she runs. But the flowers in the field have begun to turn brown, as if summer is ending too soon, and Molly is stumbling; it is she who is calling to me, "Meg, wait! Wait! I can't make it, Meg!" And there is no way I can help her.

I wake from this dream, too, in a dark and empty room from which the sound of her breathing in the next bed has gone.

I have a nightmare in which a baby is born, but is old, already, at birth. The baby looks at us, those of us who are there, with aged and tired eyes, and we realize with horror that his life is ending at the very moment of its beginning. "Why Why?" we ask, and the baby doesn't answer. Molly is there, and she is angry at our asking; she shrugs coldly and turns away from us. Only she knows the answer, and she won't share it with us, although we plead with her.

I wake terrified that it is real.

I told my father of the dreams. When I was a very little girl and had nightmares, it was always my father who came to my room when I cried out. He used to turn on the light and hold me; he showed me that the dreams weren't true.

Now he can't. We sat on the front steps in the evening, and I blew the gray fuzz of dying dandelions into the pink breeze as the sun was setting. The fears that come into my room in the night seemed far away, but Dad said, "Your dreams come out of what is real, you know. It helps, some, to think about what they mean. That you and Molly are going to be separated, even though you don't want to be. That you want to know why, why

93

life sometimes ends too soon, but no one can answer that."

I crushed the stem of a dandelion in my hand. "It doesn't help, understanding why I have nightmares. How can it help? It can't make Molly better.

"It isn't fair!" I said, the way I said it so often when I was a little girl.

"Of course it isn't fair," Dad said. "But it happens. It happens, and we have to accept that."

"And it wasn't fair that you and Mom didn't tell me!" I said, looking for someone to blame for something. "You knew all along, didn't you? You knew from the very beginning!"

He shook his head. "Meg, the doctors told us that there was a chance she would be all right. They have these medicines that they try. There is always a chance something will work. There was no way that Mom and I could tell you when there was a chance."

"Then isn't there *still* a chance?"

He shook his head slowly. "Meg, we can hope for it. We *do* hope for it. But the doctors say there isn't, now. The medicines aren't working for Molly now."

"Well, I don't believe them."

He put his arm around me and watched the sun setting.

Then he said, in his quoting voice, " 'We are such stuff as dreams are made on, and our little life is rounded with a sleep.' That's Shakespeare, Meg."

I was furious. "What did *he* know? He never knew Molly. And why *Molly?* Dad, *I'm* the one who always got into trouble! I'm the one who threw up on my own birthday cake, who broke the window in kindergarten, who stole candy from the grocery store. Molly never did anything bad!"

94

"Meg," he said. "Meg. Don't."

"I don't care," I said angrily. "Someone has got to explain to me *why*."

"It's a disease, Meg," he said in a tired voice. "A horrible, rotten disease. It just happens. There *isn't* any why."

"What's it called?" Better to know what your enemy is before you confront it, Will had told me once.

Dad sighed. "It's called 'acute myelogenous leukemia.' "

"Can you say that three times fast?" I asked him bitterly.

"Meg," said Dad, putting his arms around me and holding me so tight that his voice was muffled, "I can't even say it once. It breaks my heart."

Mom and Dad go back and forth to the hospital in Portland. They don't take me. I am too young, according to the hospital rules, to visit, but I don't think that's the reason. I think they don't want me to have to see Molly dying.

I don't argue with them. All the times I've argued with them in the past: to be allowed to see a certain movie, to drink a glass of wine with dinner, to sit in the back of one of Dad's classes at the university, listening. "I'm old enough! I'm old enough!" I remember saying. Now I don't argue, because they know and I know I'm old enough; but I'm scared. The dreams and the emptiness at home are enough; it takes all the courage I have to deal with those. I'm afraid to see my own sister, and grateful that they don't ask me to come.

When she's at home, my mother stitches on the quilt and talks about the past. Every square that she fits into place reminds her of something. She remembers Molly learning to walk, wearing the pale blue overalls that are now part of the pattern of the quilt.

"She used to fall down on her bottom, again and again," my mother smiled. "She always jumped back up laughing. Dad and I used to think sometimes that she fell on purpose, because it was funny. Molly was always looking for things to laugh at when she was a baby."

"What about me? Do you remember *me* learning to walk?"

"Of course I do," Mom said. She turned the quilt around until she found the piece she was looking for, a flowered pattern of blue and green. "This was a little dress. It was summer, and you weren't yet a year old. You were so impatient to do the things that Molly could do. I remember watching you in the back yard that summer. You were very serious and solemn, pulling yourself to your feet, trying to walk across the grass alone.

"You'd fall, and never take time to cry, or laugh, either. Your forehead would wrinkle up as you figured out how to do it right, and tried again."

"I'm like Dad."

She smiled. "Yes, you are, Meg."

"And Molly is more like you. I always thought that was an easier way to be."

Mom sighed and thought about it for a minute. "Well," she said, "it's easier for the little things, to be able to laugh at them. It makes life seem pretty simple, and a lot of fun.

"But you know, Meg," Mom said, smoothing the quilt with her fingers, "when the big, difficult things come, people like Molly and me aren't ready for them. We're so accustomed to laughing. It's harder for us when the time comes that we can't laugh."

I realized that it was the first time I had ever seen my mother not able to shrug things off with a quick smile and an easy solution. And I knew that, hard as it was for me, with my helplessness, my anger, and the dreams that came like faceless prowlers into my sleep and filled me with fear, it was worse for Mom.

"Dad and I are here, Mom," I said uncertainly, "if that helps."

"Oh, Meg," she said, and hugged me. "I don't know what I'd do without you and Dad."

10

It was five in the morning when Ben called on the third of August. Mom was in Portland, staying with friends who live near the hospital where Molly was; she and Dad were taking turns being there. It was Dad who got me up when Ben called.

I threw on my jeans and a sweater and sneakers, grabbed the camera in a big hurry, and headed across the field. It was going to be a beautiful day. The sun was coming up, very red, so that even the yellow goldenrod looked pink. The baby had obeyed Ben's instruction and elected to come in daylight. It would be a, well, a semi-obedient baby; it wouldn't wait any longer for Molly to come home. Maybe it understood the realities of things better than the rest of us.

When I knocked at their door, Ben called for me

to come on in. "I can't open it!" he called. "I'm sterile!

"I mean, I'm sterilized. Or something," he explained when I went inside and met him in the living room. He was wearing a long, white, wrinkled shirt backwards, and holding his hands up carefully so that he wouldn't touch anything.

"We blew the timing, I guess," he said, looking apologetic. "Or the book was wrong. Everything's happening faster than it was supposed to. Remember in the book, Meg, about the first stage of labor, which lasts a long time? I figured that was when we'd all be hanging around, planning what we'd do next!

"I don't know what happened. Maria just woke up about an hour ago and said she felt funny. And now, I don't know, I feel as if we ran a stoplight and ought to go back and do it again the way we were supposed to.

"I mean, I think it's going to be born right away! And I've forgotten everything the book said. I'm running around holding my sterile hands in the air, afraid to turn the pages of the book to find out what it said about the second stage. *Maria's* fine. But I feel so stupid, Meg!" He stood there, looking helpless.

I could sympathize with how he felt, because suddenly I felt panicky, and forgot how the camera worked.

"Is that Meg?" called Maria. She sounded astonishingly healthy for someone who was about to have a baby any minute. Ben went back in the room where she was, and motioned for me to follow.

She was on the bed, with her head propped up on a pillow. It didn't bother me that she was naked. We had talked about things like that enough, the three of us.

99

It bothered me a little that she was so cheerful. I thought something must be wrong; it wasn't supposed to be easy, having a baby. But Maria looked happy and full of energy. It was only Ben and I who were pale and scared.

I lifted my camera and photographed Maria smiling. The instant I had the camera in my hands, things felt comfortable. The light was good; the settings fell into place as I manipulated them; everything was okay.

Ben had a stethoscope, and he listened through Maria's abdomen to the baby. I could see that he experienced the same thing; when he picked up the simple instrument, he felt in control of things again. It was the helplessness that scared us both. "Listen!" Ben said, and handed the stethoscope to me.

I put the camera down. I listened where he told me to and could make out the rapid, strong heartbeat of the baby. It was full of energy and life; I smiled, hearing it, and nodded in response to Maria's questioning eyes.

Then, as I watched, she closed her eyes and began to breathe rapidly. I photographed her again, and turned the camera toward Ben. He was leaning over, watching carefully. I photographed the intentness of his face as he waited and watched, not touching her; she bent her knees and arched her back slightly. There was no sound in the room but her breathing, and I could see the strain move through her whole body.

"Look," Ben whispered to me. I moved to the foot of the bed, and could see, as the passage widened, taut, almost shaking with the action of the laboring muscles, the top of the baby's head. I could see its dark hair.

Then it disappeared, withdrawing like a mittened fist pulled back into a sleeve. Maria relaxed, opened her eyes, and sighed. Ben moved up near her head and talked quietly to her. "Everything's fine," he said gently. "I can see the head. It'll be soon, very soon." He smiled at her, and I photographed their heads together, and realized they had forgotten I was there.

Maria closed her eyes again and drew a deep, loud breath. Ben moved quickly again to the foot of the bed; I stood back and watched. Then I remembered the camera, moved farther from the bed, and photographed her whole body as she lay poised, gathering herself, her chin up, mouth open and gasping, waiting. Suddenly she groaned and lifted her whole body from the bed.

"Take it easy, take it easy," Ben was murmuring. He leaned forward and touched the baby's head carefully, guiding it as it moved from her body. I came closer and photographed his strong hands holding the tiny head like the shell of an egg. The face was toward me, flat and motionless, its features nothing more than lines like a hastily drawn cartoon: the straight line of a motionless mouth, two slits of swollen, tightly closed eyes, and the tiny, squashed curve of a nose. Maria relaxed again. Ben stood very still, his hands still gently around the head, and the small, flattened face was as immobile as the painted face of a plastic toy.

"Once more," he told Maria. I don't think she heard him at all; her whole being was clenched tight, and then she gasped as the rest of the little body slid toward Ben.

And still the only sound was Maria breathing. I was shooting pictures but I didn't even hear the click of the shutter, just the long, quiet, exhausted breaths.

Then, the cry of the child. Ben was holding it there in his two hands, rubbing it between them.

He rubbed its narrow, grayish back; finally, the incredibly small arms and legs moved a little, like a sleeper startled from a dream, and it wailed briefly. Maria smiled at the sound and lifted her head to see. Ben grinned at her and said, "It's a boy. I told you it would be a boy."

He lay the baby on her stomach, waited a moment, and then tied the cord in two places and cut carefully between them. The baby was free of Maria now, but it squirmed against her as if it wanted to stay close. Its face, in those few moments, had changed from bluish-gray to pink, and like a sponge dipped in water, a shape had grown from the flatness of it. The tiny nose had risen into a soft and perfect curve; the thin line of mouth had become a moving, searching thing, and a tongue came from between the lips, tasting the air; the eyes opened and closed, blinking and squinting; the forehead drew up into wrinkles as the head turned against Maria's skin. She reached down with one hand, touched it gently, and smiled. Then she closed her eyes and rested again.

"Meg?" Ben handed me a soft white towel from the pile of things he had on a table beside him. "Take the baby for a few minutes, would you, while I finish up here?"

I put my camera on the floor in the corner, wrapped the towel around the baby, and lifted it away from Maria. It was so tiny, so light. I pushed the towel away from the little face, and held it down so Maria could see. She smiled at me, murmured, "Thank you," and I took the baby into the living room.

I held him for a moment in the open front doorway of the house. The sun was golden now, and the dew was already evaporating from the tall grass and flowers in the field. The birds were awake. "Listen," I whispered to the baby, "the birds are singing to you." But he was asleep, his fingers relaxed and warm against my chest.

I sat in the rocking chair and moved slowly back and forth, trying with the soft, steady rhythm of the chair to make up for the abrupt and agonizing journey he had just had. I thought of the overwhelming force that had gripped Maria's whole being at his birth, and the startled, almost painful way that he had moved as he felt his way to life outside her body. I was shaken more than I had anticipated by the awesomeness of the transition.

With one hand I took a corner of the towel and wiped his face, which was still stained from his delivery. As the towel touched him, he gave a surprised jerk and opened both eyes; his fingers fluttered. Then he fell asleep again, breathing softly. The corners of his mouth moved briefly into what seemed to be a momentary smile, and he made a little sound with his lips as he slept.

"Ben?" I called softly.

"Yes? Everything okay? I'm almost through."

"Everything's fine. He says to tell you he's happy."

Ben came out of the room where Maria was, wiping his hands on a towel. He leaned over me, looked down at the baby, and grinned. "He says he's happy? I *told* you he'd tell us his name."

I gave the baby to Ben, went in the bedroom to get my camera, and kissed Maria on the cheek. She was covered with a blanket, and sleeping. I left the three of them there by themselves, and went back home to where my father was waiting.

And they did name him Happy. Happy William Abbott-Brady. When Will Banks heard that, he was a little taken aback at first. "Happy William?" he asked in surprise. "What kind of name

103

is *that?*" Then he thought for a moment. "Well, there's a flower called *Sweet* William. *Dianthus barbatus*, actually. So I suppose there's no reason why a boy can't be named Happy William. So long as he lives up to it, of course."

Suddenly I wanted to be the one to tell Molly.

I had been afraid to see Molly, and now I wasn't. There isn't any way to explain that. The only thing that had happened was that I had watched Maria give birth to Happy, and for some reason that made a difference.

Dad drove me to Portland, and on the way he tried to tell me what it would be like at the hospital. "You have to keep reminding yourself," he said, "that it's still Molly. That's the hard thing, for me. Every time I go in her room, it takes me by surprise, seeing all that machinery. It seems to separate you from her. You have to look past it, and see that it's still Molly. Do you understand?"

I shook my head. "No," I said.

Dad sighed. "Well, I'm not sure I do either. But listen, Meg—when you think of Molly, how do you think of her?"

I was quiet for a minute, thinking. "I guess mostly I think of how she used to laugh. And then I think of how, even after she got sick, she used to run out in the field on sunny mornings, looking for new flowers. I used to watch her, sometimes, from the window."

"That's what I mean. That's the way I think of Molly, too. But when you get to the hospital, you'll see that everything is different for Molly now. It will make you feel strange, because you're outside of it; you're not part of it.

"She'll be very sleepy. That's because of the drugs they're giving her, so that she'll feel comfortable. And she can't talk to you, because there's a tube in her throat to help her breathe.

"She'll look like a stranger to you, at first. And it'll be scary. But she can hear you, Meg. Talk to her. And you'll realize that underneath all that stuff, the tubes and needles and medicines, our Molly is still there. You have to remember that. It makes it easier.

"And, Meg?" He was driving very carefully, following the white line in the center of the curving road.

"What?"

"One more thing. Remember, too, that Molly's not in any pain, and she's not scared. It's only you and I and Mom, now, who are hurting and frightened.

"This is a hard thing to explain, Meg, but Molly is handling this thing very well by herself. She needs us, for our love, but she doesn't need us for anything else now." He swallowed hard and said, "Dying is a very solitary thing. The only thing we can do is be there when she wants us there."

I had brought the little vase of pussy willows with me. I shifted them on my lap, and reached over and squeezed Dad's hand for a minute.

Mom met us at the hospital; the three of us had lunch together in the first-floor coffee shop. We talked mostly about Happy.

"I was the first one to hold him, Mom," I told her. "I think he smiled at me."

Mom looked as if she was remembering something. She started to speak, stopped and was silent for a minute, and then said what she had been thinking. "I remember when Molly was born. It's a very special time."

She told me that Molly was awake, that she knew I was coming, that she wanted me there. Then they took me upstairs.

She looked so small. For the first time in my life I felt older, bigger than Molly.

But not more beautiful. I would never feel more beautiful than Molly.

Her hair was completely gone. All those long blond curls were no longer part of Molly; the translucent skin of her face and head were like the fine china of an antique doll against the white pillow of the hospital bed. Above her, labeled glass bottles and plastic bags dangled from a metal rack; through the tubes that led from them to the veins in Molly's left arm, I watched the solutions drip slowly, like tears. The tube that entered her throat was held firmly in place with clean adhesive tape against her skin. I tried to separate all those things from Molly in my mind. Even though pain was knotted inside me like a fist, I saw the way the lashes of her closed eyes were outlined on her cheek in perfect curving lines; I followed with my eyes the moving, blurred patterns of sunshine from the window on her bed, as the leaves of the trees outside moved and swept the sun across her hands and arms.

"Molly," I said. She opened her eyes, found me there, and smiled. She waited for me to talk to her.

"Molly, the baby is born."

She smiled again, very sleepily.

"It's a boy. He was born in the brass bed, the way they wanted. He came very quickly. Ben was all set to wait for hours, but Maria kept laughing and saying, 'No, Ben, it's coming right away!' And it did. Ben picked him up and put him on Maria's stomach, and he curled up and went to sleep."

She was watching me, listening. For a moment it was as if we were home again, in our beds, talking in the dark.

"Then Ben gave him to me, and I carried him to the doorway and showed him that the sun was coming up. I told him the birds were singing to him.

"Will came over later and brought them a big bouquet of wild flowers, I don't know the names— you would, though. All yellow and white.

"Ben and Maria and Will all said to tell you they love you."

She reached out and took my hand and squeezed it. Her hand was not as strong as Happy's.

"Ben and Maria asked me if I would make another copy of the picture of you holding the Queen Anne's lace. They want to hang it on the wall in the living room."

But she wasn't listening anymore. She had turned her head to one side and closed her eyes. Her hand slipped gently out of mine and she was asleep again. I put the little vase of pussy willows on the table beside her bed, where she would see it when she woke up. Then I left her there alone.

On the drive home, I told my father, "Will Banks said a line from a poem to me once. He said, 'It is Margaret you mourn for,' and I told him I never mourn for myself. But I think he was right. So much of my sadness is because I miss Molly. I even miss fighting with her."

My father pulled me over close to him on the seat of the car and put his arm around me. "You've been great through all of this, Meg," he said. "I'm sorry I haven't told you that before. I've been busy mourning for myself too."

Then we sang the rest of the way home. We sang "Michael, Row Your Boat Ashore," mostly off-key and we made up verses for everybody. We sang "Dad's boat is a Book boat," "Mom's boat is Quilt boat," "Meg's boat is a Camera boat," "Ben and Maria's boat is a Happy boat," and "Will's boat is

107

a House boat," which struck us both as much funnier than it really was. Finally, we sang "Molly's boat is a Flower boat," and when we finished that verse, we were turning down the dirt road to home.

Two weeks later she was gone. She just closed her eyes one afternoon and didn't ever open them again. Mom and Dad brought the pussy willows back for me to keep.

11

Time goes on, and your life is still there, and you have to live it. After a while you remember the good things more often than the bad. Then, gradually, the empty silent parts of you fill up with sounds of talking and laughter again, and the jagged edges of sadness are softened by memories.

Nothing will be the same, ever, without Molly. But there's a whole world waiting, still, and there are good things in it.

It was September, and time to leave the little house that had begun to seem like home.

I answered the knock at the front door and then went upstairs to the study. Dad was sitting at his desk, just staring gloomily at the piles of paperclipped pages that he had arranged in some order on the floor.

"Dad, Clarice Callaway is at the door with some man. She says she hates to bother you at such a bad time, but."

"But she is going to do it anyway, right?" He sighed and got up. At the front door I heard Clarice introducing him to the man who was standing there holding a briefcase and looking impatient and annoyed. Dad brought them inside, asked Mom to make some coffee, and the three of them sat down in the living room.

I went back to the darkroom where I was trying to pack. I was going to have a darkroom in town; Dad had already hired a couple of his students to build the shelves and do the plumbing and wiring in what had been a maid's room, many years ago, on the third floor of the house there. It would, in fact, be a larger, better equipped darkroom than the one I'd had all summer, so it wasn't that that was making me depressed. And Will Banks had almost completed work on the darkroom that he was building for himself, in what had been a pantry of his little house. So my going away wasn't going to mean the end of Will's interest and enthusiasm or skill, and it couldn't have been that that was making me feel sad as I packed up my negatives and chemicals and tools. I guess it was just that we wouldn't be doing it together anymore, Will and I.

It is hard to give up the being together with someone.

I sealed the packing boxes with tape, wrote "Darkroom" on them, and carried them to a corner of the kitchen. There were other boxes there already; Mom had been packing for several days. There were boxes marked "Dishes," "Cooking Utensils," and "Linens." We'd been living like campers all week, eating from paper plates, finishing up the odds and ends in the refrigerator, making meals from the last few things in Mom's little garden.

There was a box marked "Quilt." Two nights before, my mother had snapped off a thread, looked at the quilt in surprise, and said, "I think it's finished. How can it be finished?" She turned it all around, looking for some corner or spot that she'd forgotten, but every inch was covered with the neat, close-together rows of her tiny stitches. She stood up and laid it out on the big kitchen table. There they were, all those orderly, geometric patterns of our past, Molly's and mine. All those bright squares of color: in the center, the pale pinks and yellows of our baby dresses; farther out, in carefully organized rows, the little flowery prints and the bright plaids of the years when we were little girls; and at the edges, the more subdued and faded denims and corduroys of our growing up.

"It really is," she said slowly. "It's all done." Then she folded it and put it in the box.

Now I could hear her serving coffee in the living room. There was an argument going on. I could hear the quick, angry voices of the visitors, and suddenly I heard my mother's soft voice say, "That's not *fair*," the way I had so often said the same thing to Molly.

There was silence in the living room for a moment after Mom said that. Then I heard my father say, "There's no point in our continuing to discuss this. Let's go down the road to see Will. You should have gone to see him first, Mr. Huntington."

Dad came into the kitchen to use the phone. "Will?" he said. "Your nephew is here. Can we come down?"

Dad grinned as he listened to the reply. I could imagine what Will was saying; I had never heard him say a good word about his sister's son.

111

"Will," said Dad on the phone. "*You* know that, and *I* know that. Nevertheless, we have to be civilized. Now calm down. We'll be there in a few minutes."

After he hung up, he said to me, "Meg, run over to Ben and Maria's, would you? Tell them you'll stay with Happy if they'll meet us at Will's house to talk to his nephew from Boston."

When he went back into the living room, I heard Clarice Callaway say, "I haven't finished my coffee."

And I heard my father reply, "Clarice, I hate to inconvenience you, but." I could tell from his voice that it gave him a lot of satisfaction, saying it.

I loved taking care of Happy. That was another thing I hated about moving back to town, that I wouldn't have a chance to watch him grow bigger and learn things. Already he was holding his head up and looking around. The newborn baby part of him was already in the past, after only a month; now he was a little person, with big eyes, a loud voice, and a definite personality. Maria said he was like Ben, with a screwball sense of humor and no respect for propriety. Ben said he was like Maria: illogical, assertive, and a showoff. Maria whacked Ben with a dish towel when he said that, and Ben grinned and said, "See what I mean?"

I just thought he was Happy, not like anyone else but himself.

When Ben and Maria came back from Will's, I asked them what was going on. Maria rolled her eyes and said, "*I* don't know. Craziness, that's what's going on."

Ben was roaring with laughter. "Meg, I have to show you something." He went to the closet and got the box with the album of wedding pictures.

"I've already seen them, Ben. I know you're

112

married. I told my father so. Clarice can't still be worrying about *that*."

"No, no, *look*, dummy," said Ben. He flipped through the heavy pages of colored photographs until he found the one he wanted. It was of a crowd of wedding guests, middle-aged people, drinking champagne. In the center of the crowd, looking terribly proper and at the same time a little silly from the champagne, was Will Banks' nephew.

"It's Martin Huntington!" Ben was practically doubled up, laughing. "I couldn't believe it. I walked into Will's house, and there was this jerk with a lawyer suit on, holding a briefcase, and he looked at me with my jeans and my beard, as if he didn't want to get too close for fear of being infected with some disease. And when I realized who he was, I held out my hand—you should have been there, Meg—and said, 'Mr. Huntington, don't you remember me? I'm Ben Brady.' "

"How do you know *him?*" I asked.

"He's been a junior partner in my father's law firm for years," laughed Ben. "Oh, you should have seen it, Meg. He stood there in Will's living room with his mouth open, and then he said in that pompous way he has, "Well, Benjamin. I, ah, of course had no idea that, ah, it was you living in my family's house. Ah, of course, this does, ah, add a certain element of, ah, awkwardness to these proceedings.'

" 'Proceedings!' Can you imagine, calling a discussion in Will Banks' living room 'proceedings'? That's so typical of Martin Huntington. I can't wait to tell my father!"

"But what's going to happen?"

Ben shrugged. "I don't know. But I'm going to call my father. I know what I'd like to have happen. I'd like to buy this house from Will, if my dad will lend me the money for a down payment.

I'd like Happy to grow up here. How about that, Hap? Hey, Maria, doesn't that kid ever stop eating?"

Maria was nursing Happy. She grinned at Ben. "He's gonna take after his old man," she said.

Back home, my parents were in the living room drinking the reheated coffee. The rug was rolled up, and the curtains were gone from the windows. Little by little the house was being emptied of everything that had been ours.

"Ben wants to buy the house," I told them. "And they'd live here always." I sighed, kicked off my shoes, and brushed away the pieces of dead leaves that were stuck to my socks and jeans. Everything in the field seemed to be dying.

"Well, that's terrific!" said my father. "Why are you looking so glum?"

"I'm not sure," I answered. "I guess because we're leaving. Next summer everything will be the same for *them*, but what about us?"

Mom and Dad were quiet for a minute. Finally Dad said, "Listen, Meg. This house will still be here next summer. We *could* rent it again. But Mom and I have talked about it, and we're just not sure."

"There are so many sad memories for us here, Meg," my mother said quietly.

"By next summer, though," I suggested, "maybe it would be easier. Maybe it would be fun to remember Molly in this house."

Mom smiled. "Maybe. We'll wait and see."

The three of us stood up; Mom headed for the kitchen, to finish the packing there. Dad started up the stairs to his study.

"You know," he said, stopping halfway up the staircase. "At one point in the book, I wrote that the use of coincidence is an immature literary de-

114

vice. But when Ben walked into Will's living room today and said, 'Mr. Huntington, don't you remember me?,' well—"

He stood there thinking for a moment. Then he started talking to himself.

"If I rearranged the ninth chapter," he muttered, "to make it correspond to—" He walked slowly up the rest of the stairs, muttering. At the top of the stairs he stood, looking into the study at the piles of pages, then turned and called down to us triumphantly, "Lydia! Meg! The book is *finished!* It only needs rearranging! I didn't realize it until now!"

So the manuscript was packed, too, and in great bold capital letters, Dad wrote on the box, "BOOK."

The next day, the moving van came. Will Banks, Ben, and Maria, holding Happy, stood in the driveway of the little house, and waved good-bye.

It was the end of September when my father came home after his classes one day and told me, "Meg, comb your hair. I want you to go someplace with me."

Usually he doesn't notice or care if my hair is combed, so I knew it was someplace special. I even washed my face and changed from sneakers into my school shoes. I grabbed a jacket—it was getting chilly: the kind of September air that smells of pumpkins, apples, and dead leaves—and got into the car. Dad drove me to the university museum, the big stone building with bronze statues in front of it.

"Dad," I whispered as we went up the wide steps, "I have seen the Renaissance collection a thousand times. If you're going to make me take that guided tour *again*, I'll—"

"Meg," he said. "Will you please hush?"

The lady at the front desk knew Dad. "Dr. Chalmers," she said, "I was so sorry to hear about your daughter."

"Thank you," said my father. "This is my other daughter, Meg. Meg, this is Miss Amato."

I shook her hand, and she looked at me curiously. "Oh," she said, as if she were surprised. Didn't she know that Dad had another daughter? *"Oh,"* she said again. "The photography exhibition is in the west wing, Dr. Chalmers."

I hadn't even heard about a photography exhibition. Not surprising, because I'd been so busy, fixing up the new darkroom, and getting ready for school. I had a sudden sinking feeling as Dad and I walked toward the west wing.

"Dad," I said, "you didn't submit any of my photographs to an exhibition, did you?"

"No," he said, shaking his head. "I would never have done that without asking your permission, Meg. Someday you'll do that yourself."

The huge white-walled room was filled with framed photographs on each wall. The sign at the entrance to the room was carefully lettered in Gothic script: *Faces of New England.* As I walked around the room, I recognized the names of many of the photographers: famous names, names I had seen in magazines and in books of photographs that I had taken from the library. The photographs were all of people: the old, gaunt faces of farmers who live on the back roads; the weathered, wrinkled faces of their wives; the eager-eyed, sunshine-speckled faces of children.

And suddenly there was my face. It was a large photograph, against a white mount, framed in a narrow black frame, and it was not just the coincidence of a stranger who happened to look like me; it was my face. It was taken at an angle; the wind was blowing my hair, and I was looking off in the distance somewhere, far beyond the meticulously trimmed edges of the photograph or the rigid confines of its frame. The outline of my neck and chin and half-turned cheek were sharp against the blurred and subtle shapes of pine trees in the background.

I knew, though I had not known it then, that Will had taken it. He had taken it in the village cemetery the day we buried Molly there and heaped her grave with goldenrod.

There was something of Molly in my face. It startled me, seeing it. The line that defined my face, the line that separated the darkness of the trees from the light that curved into my forehead and cheek was the same line that had once identified Molly by its shape. The way I held my shoulders was the way she had held hers. It was a transient thing, I knew, but when Will had held the camera and released the shutter of one five-hundredth of a second, he had captured it and made permanent whatever of Molly was in me. I was grateful, and glad.

I went close to read what was written below the photograph. The title was "Fringed Gentian"; on the other side was his signature: *William Banks*.

"Dad," I said, "I have to go back. I have to see Will. I promised him."

My father took me back on the weekend. I remembered, in the car, what a long trip it had seemed last winter, when we went for the first time to the house in the country. Now the distance seemed short. Perhaps it is part of a place becoming familiar that makes it seem closer; perhaps it is just a part of growing up.

There was Will, with his head inside the open hood of his truck. He stood up straight when we

117

drove in, wiped his hands, and chuckled, "Spark plugs."

"Will, I came so you could show me the fringed gentian. I'm sorry I forgot."

"You didn't forget, Meg," he told me. "It wasn't time until now."

My father waited at Will's house while we walked across the fields. Almost all of the flowers were gone. Ben and Maria's house was closed up tight and empty, although the curtains Maria had made still hung at the windows. They had gone back so that Ben could complete the last course for his master's degree at Harvard.

"They'll be back," said Will, watching me look at the house, with its paint still new and its garden still tidy and weeded, even though the vegetables were gone. "The house is theirs now. Maybe next summer you can help Happy learn to walk."

Maybe. Maybe there would be another summer filled with flowers and the laughter of a little boy whose life was still brand-new.

Will went right to the place on the side of the woods where the spruce tree was beside the birches. I had forgotten the spot that he had pointed out months before, but this was his land; he knew it like his life. He pushed aside the underbrush and led me to the place where he knew the gentians would be growing. It was very quiet there. The ground was mostly moss, and the sunlight came down through the tall trees in patches, lighting the deep green here and there in patterns like the patchwork of a quilt.

The little clump of fringed gentians stood alone, the purple blossoms at the tops of straight stems that grew up toward the sunlight from the damp earth. Will and I stood and looked at them together.

118

"They're my favorite flower," he told me, "I suppose because they're the last of the season. And because they grow here all alone, not caring whether anyone sees them or not."

"They're beautiful, Will," I said; and they were.

" 'It tried to be a rose,' " Will said, and I knew he was quoting again, " 'and failed, and all the summer laughed: but just before the snows there came a purple creature that ravished all the hill; and summer hid her forehead, and mockery was still.' "

"Will," I said, as we turned to leave the woods, "you should have been a poet."

He laughed. "A truck mechanic would have been more practical."

I fell a little way behind him as we walked back across the field, wanting to capture every image in my mind. Even the goldenrod was gone. The tall grasses had turned brownish and brittle, like the sepia tones of an old and faded photograph. In my mind, in quick sequences as if a film were stopping and starting, I saw Molly again. I saw her standing in the grass when it was green, her arms full of flowers; with the wind in her hair, with her quick smile, reaching for the next flower, and the next. The floating pollen drifted in patterns through the sunlight around her, as she looked back over her shoulder, laughing.

Somewhere, for Molly, I thought suddenly, it would be summer still, summer always.

Across the field I saw the little house that had been our house. And ahead of me I saw Will. I watched as he walked toward home, pushing the grass aside with his heavy stick, and realized that he was leaning on it as he walked, that he needed its support. Walking through the rocky field wasn't as easy for him as it was for me. I understood then what Ben had told me once, about knowing

119

and accepting that bad things will happen, because I understood, watching him, that someday Will would be gone from me too.

I ran to catch up. "Will," I said, "do you know that the picture of me is hanging in the university museum?"

He nodded. "Do you mind?"

I shook my head. "You made me beautiful," I said shyly.

"Meg," he laughed, putting one arm over my shoulders, "you were beautiful all along."

ABOUT THE AUTHOR

Born in Honolulu, Hawaii, LOIS LOWRY lived all over the world—Tokyo, New York City, Cambridge, Massachusetts—before she settled permanently in rural Maine in a house that is overrun with an assortment of dogs, cats and children. She has continued to lead a peripatetic life, working as a freelance journalist and as a photographer specializing in portraits of children. Recently the same month saw her in New York photographing children and hitchhiking around Nova Scotia interviewing lobster fishermen for a newspaper article. *A Summer to Die* is Lowry's first book for children. Though the book is not autobiographical, facing the death of her only sister when she was young made it possible for her to write about the subject with a good deal of personal understanding. In addition, Lois Lowry's professional experience in photography becomes an integral part of the book.

TEENAGERS FACE LIFE AND LOVE

Choose books filled with fun and adventure, discovery and disenchantment, failure and conquest, triumph and tragedy, life and love.

☐	12033	**THE LATE GREAT ME** Sandra Scoppettone	$1.75
☐	10946	**HOME BEFORE DARK** Sue Ellen Bridgers	$1.50
☐	11961	**THE GOLDEN SHORES OF HEAVEN** Katie Letcher Lyle	$1.50
☐	12501	**PARDON ME, YOU'RE STEPPING ON MY EYEBALL!** Paul Zindel	$1.95
☐	11091	**A HOUSE FOR JONNIE O.** Blossom Elfman	$1.95
☐	12025	**ONE FAT SUMMER** Robert Lipsyte	$1.75
☐	12252	**I KNOW WHY THE CAGED BIRD SINGS** Maya Angelou	$1.95
☐	11800	**ROLL OF THUNDER, HEAR MY CRY** Mildred Taylor	$1.75
☐	12741	**MY DARLING, MY HAMBURGER** Paul Zindel	$1.95
☐	10370	**THE BELL JAR** Sylvia Plath	$1.95
☐	12338	**WHERE THE RED FERN GROWS** Wilson Rawls	$1.75
☐	11829	**CONFESSIONS OF A TEENAGE BABOON** Paul Zindel	$1.95
☐	11632	**MARY WHITE** Caryl Ledner	$1.95
☐	11640	**SOMETHING FOR JOEY** Richard E. Peck	$1.75
☐	12347	**SUMMER OF MY GERMAN SOLDIER** Bette Greene	$1.75
☐	11839	**WINNING** Robin Brancato	$1.75
☐	12057	**IT'S NOT THE END OF THE WORLD** Judy Blume	$1.50